One night. It was only meant to be one night.

Genie only realized she'd said it out loud when Seve's whole body tightened, turning even more marble-like than before.

"Why are you doing this? You don't even want a child. You said as much when we had dinner."

His eyes glinted, his incisive gaze tracking her as she paced in the small cabin. "What I felt a few weeks ago no longer matters."

"That's absurd. Of course it does."

He gritted his teeth. "Let me rephrase. The child you're carrying—*my* child—is now my number one priority. I'm not taking my eyes off you until he or she is born."

Maya Blake's hopes of becoming a writer were born when she picked up her first romance at thirteen. Little did she know her dream would come true! Does she still pinch herself every now and then to make sure it's not a dream? Yes, she does! Feel free to pinch her, too, via Twitter, Facebook or Goodreads! Happy reading!

Books by Maya Blake

Harlequin Presents

The Greek's Hidden Vows
Reclaimed for His Royal Bed
The Greek's Forgotten Marriage

Brothers of the Desert

Their Desert Night of Scandal
His Pregnant Desert Queen

Ghana's Most Eligible Billionaires

Bound by Her Rival's Baby
A Vow to Claim His Hidden Son

Visit the Author Profile page
at Harlequin.com for more titles.

Maya Blake

PREGNANT AND STOLEN
BY THE TYCOON

ISBN-13: 978-1-335-59296-5

Pregnant and Stolen by the Tycoon

Copyright © 2023 by Maya Blake

Recycling programs
for this product may
not exist in your area.

For questions and comments about the quality of this book,
please contact us at CustomerService@Harlequin.com.

Harlequin Enterprises ULC
22 Adelaide St. West, 41st Floor
Toronto, Ontario M5H 4E3, Canada
www.Harlequin.com

Printed in U.S.A.

PREGNANT AND STOLEN
BY THE TYCOON

CHAPTER ONE

'SEND THE NEXT ONE IN, Lily. Please.'

Genie Merchant remembered to tag on the courtesy, despite her brain firing off in a million tangential directions.

Social cues are important.

Her childhood therapist's words echoed at the back of her head.

Why? she remembered asking.

A wry smile from wise eyes.

They oil the wheels of evolution.

She remembered silently snorting back then. That sound, too, echoed at the back of her mind now. No number of courteous words tagged onto hard facts and sophisticated, ground-breaking coding had been enough to secure her what she wanted.

Instead, it'd only resulted in drawing unwanted attention from men in suits who wanted to steal years of her hard work.

Her *life's* work.

Which was why she was reduced to this…farce.

Why she'd swapped her favourite lounging co-ords and Ugg boots for a cream jumpsuit, uncomfortable heels, and itchy jewellery the online stylist called 'on trend'. Why she'd exchanged her utilitarian glasses for contacts that made her blink like an electrocuted owl, left the sanctuary of her basement tech lab and home, and travelled up to the twenty-first floor of the building overlooking the east London ribbon of the Thames.

She barely looked up to catch her assistant's reserved smile as the woman nodded and stepped back out of her office.

Four meetings down, one to go.

Four *very disappointing* meetings.

She was running out of time. At her last check on the dark web this morning, there were six questionable entities closing in on her, ready to force her hand or take her intellectual property by force, two of them security forces of so-called democracies.

She had a week, maybe ten days, at most.

And if she was successful…

Genie sucked in a long, shaky breath, attempting not to dwell on that thought. But it was no use. With her dream tantalisingly close, it was impossible not to skim past it one more time. Maybe even to linger longingly for a few seconds.

To imagine what it would *feel* like to—

'Mr Graham to see you, Miss Merchant.'

Genie schooled her features and posture into the stance she'd wasted precious time perfecting in front of the mirror this morning and turned.

Shoulders back. Steady eye contact. Lips stretched a half-inch on either side but no showing of teeth. Hand outstretched ninety degrees from her body.

'Mr Graham. Thank you for coming.'

The short, thin man with small, beady eyes looked her up and down. 'No, thank *you* for making the time to see me. And call me Frank.' His toothy smile stretched even wider as he blatantly appraised her. 'Had I known what a vision you were, I would've reached out much earlier.'

Her reservations, already severely tested from having to go down this road, hardened into rejection as his sweaty hand grasped hers and subtly tugged her closer.

She resisted and pulled away from him to link her fingers in front of her. 'I hope my gender isn't the determining factor of our negotiations?' she enquired, her cold tone icing between them.

He eyed her in wary surprise, before he laughed. 'Of course not, Genie. May I call you Genie?'

'No. Miss Merchant will be quite adequate. Thank you.'

His face dropped and her ire rose. Was he really that deluded? Did he believe this was a social exercise? That sexist informality was his gateway to acquiring her most prized possession?

She watched him examine her office, taking in the stark icy blue minimalist decor with faint disdain before lingering for several seconds on the velvet grey sofa.

'Well, shall we make ourselves comfortable, Genie?' he asked, his American twang thickening as he waved her towards the sofa instead of the small conference table she'd opted to use for her other meetings.

His blithe refusal of her request stiffened her spine and made up her mind. 'No. I don't think this is going to work, Mr Graham.'

His face morphed from condescension to anger. 'Excuse me? You haven't even heard my offer.'

'Do you even understand how my algorithm works?' The beauty of her highly sophisticated predictive algorithm was that it could work wonders for a farmer in Peru in accurately projecting weather patterns, long term soil viability and a plethora of advantages. The bad news was that in the wrong hands, it could also be weaponised to give military advantage to a ruthless dictator. Hence her being at pains to ensure it didn't fall into the wrong hands.

He shrugged. 'Not in its entirety, but I have a few dozen clever geeks back in Silicon Valley who are very excited about it and ready to put it to great use. So why don't we talk numbers?'

'No.' She considered the social cue. Then disregarded it. Frank Graham didn't deserve her *thanks for coming*. He'd wasted her time. Precious time she'd never recoup.

Anger reddened his face. 'Now, look here. I flew in from California especially for this meeting. You can't just dismiss me without hearing me—'

'I can and I just have.' Striding to her desk, she pressed the button for her secretary, then another one that automated her office door.

It swung smoothly open, and Genie breathed a sigh of relief to see the two burly guards standing in the doorway.

Yes, she had been reduced to employing bodyguards because in moments like these, and as she'd discovered in the last six months, it was effective in deterring the men in suits who didn't have qualms about taking what was hers.

Frank Graham looked ready to force the issue, until he saw the security and changed his mind. It didn't stop him from sneering, 'Little girls who think they can play in a man's world get what's coming to them, eventually. Mark my words.'

'I won't. In fact, I've already forgotten them. Good day, Mr Graham.'

She kept her posture and her expression intact despite the knot of despair tightening in her stomach. But the moment the door shut behind the odious man, she sagged into her chair, then twisted it around to stare unseeing out of the window.

She registered neither the tourist boat floating lazily down the river nor the unseasonably bright blue skies overhead. Neither the acrobat entertaining passers-by on his tiny unicycle nor the group of young students sharing a joke over their lunch.

But the young mother pushing a stylish little pram caught her eye. Pulled agonisingly hard on her heart-strings.

Her dream. Her one wish. Now even farther away than it'd been this morning.

Her posture deflated further until Genie suspected she could disappear into the giant chair she hated but which the decorator had insisted was the right symbol to project power and dominance.

Genie had declined to point out that she didn't need outward trappings to demonstrate her worth. Her power and dominance came from her superior brain power. Her Rhodes Scholar accolades and the Girl Genius label the media liked to crow about, despite her being twenty-eight instead of eight, spoke volumes for themselves.

She should've taken her business team's advice and let them broker this deal on her behalf. But wouldn't that have been more painful than putting herself through the torture of social confrontation with strangers? Wouldn't sitting in her lab downstairs, blissfully surrounded by her super computers and out of the way but having othoro decide on the fate of her life's work, have been even more excruciating?

A breath shuddered out of her, her forlorn gaze resting on the mother who'd paused to coo at her baby and following them until they were out of view.

Yes, it would've been excruciating, but she wouldn't be here, taking a front-row seat to her own failure.

Affirm the positive. Don't dwell on the negative.

This time her snort ripped free, tinged by a dart of guilt.

Dr Douglas wouldn't have approved. He would've called it 'an unfortunate social miscue'.

But Dr Douglas had retired a long time ago, and then shortly after that, her Christmas card had been 'returned to sender' because he'd passed away.

She was on her own. Alone and circling the drain of failure.

The soft whine of her door made her grit her teeth. Was she to be denied even this rare moment of self-pity?

'We're done for the day, Lily.' She scrambled through her morose thoughts and summoned further socially accepted words for her assistant. 'I am...grateful for your help. We did, however, fall far short of our goals, so—'

'Don't be ready to throw in the towel just yet, Miss Merchant.'

Genie swivelled around at the sound of the voice.

The deep rumbling volcano of a voice.

Not hyperbole.

The man striding with supreme confidence into her office had the voice that could rival the soundtrack of that volcano that had erupted in Hawaii recently. And it was accented. Not thick but blended with something else. Enough to make it distinctive.

South America. Spanish. But not quite Chile. Not quite Argentina. Off the coast. Smoke. Fire. *Samba.*

'Cardosia,' she murmured.

He paused, his eyes narrowing a fraction, then gleaming, before he inclined his head. 'Indeed. Not many can tell.'

Genie shrugged. 'I can parse thirty-seven languages and dialects.' She wasn't entirely certain why she felt the need to share that information and on some level she knew she would be disappointed when she arrived at the reason why. Because it strongly suggested she was intimidated by this stranger.

This towering force moving through her personal space.

She tilted her head and examined him clinically.

He was hands down the finest male specimen she'd ever seen. Considering she rarely left her building, she might be sorely lacking in source material with which to compare him, but if she placed him in the category assigned by her favourite TV characters, he was a 'banging ten-ten studly stud'.

Had he taken a wrong turn to a photoshoot for those far too large billboards that dominated the skyline and seemed to slap her in the face whenever she ventured out? Because he really was too much to behold.

She looked past him to her assistant. 'Lily.' The older woman had worked for Merchant Labs long enough to decode the question held within her name.

'I'm sorry, Miss Merchant, I don't have Mr...um...'

'Severino Valente,' the stranger supplied, the intensity of his voice deepening further.

Lily's eyes widened, then her face flushed. Genie categorised the reaction and deduced that her assistant had registered the 'studly-studness' of her unwanted visitor.

'I don't have Mr Valente on the schedule, but he said you'd be interested in taking this meeting with him, and since Mr Graham left early...'

Genie kept her gaze on Lily, faintly registering that perhaps she was staring too long, perhaps even displaying her displeasure with this uncharacteristic action by her assistant. Was that...fair or unfair? 'Did he?'

Diverting her attention from Lily, she met a pair of unwavering slate-grey eyes, her question, also meant to ridicule his assumption, bouncing off his wide shoulders.

He moved towards her, and the most peculiar thing happened.

Her skin began to tighten. Not in flight-or-fight mode. She knew those two well enough. Had experienced both in the past six months and beyond that in the not so distant past, when she'd questioned her true value to the people who should've cared about her. When she'd believed she might be better off on her own.

No, this was different.

It felt almost like...anticipation. *Stimulation.* Although why she should...*oh.*

Oh. Goodness.

Her body was straining towards him of its own volition. And her hand was extending towards his in answer to the large one he held out to her.

As if he had some sort of...*power* over her.

Alpha-male posturing.

She'd read that somewhere. The logical thing to do to negate stimulus was to separate the stimulant from the object. She started to drop her hand, even contemplated stepping back but that would be a red flag he wouldn't miss.

'My assistant is correct that my last meeting was cut short. But I'm afraid I don't have time for another, especially with someone who walked in off the street.'

He dropped his hand and Genie felt an odd disquiet that he hadn't pushed for a handshake. 'I'm not a random visitor, Miss Merchant. My people have been trying to set up a meeting with you for weeks.'

'Then that should've been a firm indicator that I wasn't interested in whatever this is about.'

He shoved his hand into his expensive coat pocket, the action widening the gap between the lapels to show the bespoke suit he wore underneath. The dark navy shirt threw his deep olive complexion into strong focus, emphasising every masculine feature he possessed. 'If I were in the habit of allowing every small hurdle to stop me, I wouldn't be where I am today.'

Genie wasn't sure whether she bristled at the 'small' or the 'hurdle' part.

Before she could respond, he continued, 'Besides, I have it on good authority that your initial short list has been a total failure. Perhaps you should rethink the parameters of your selection.'

'I don't need advice on how I conduct my business, Mr Valente. *My* people will be compiling the next list. Feel free to speak with them, although I can't guarantee you'll be successful next time either.'

He sauntered past her as if she hadn't spoken, prowling to the very window she'd been staring out of a few minutes ago. After a charged minute—which she spent far too engrossed in his riveting profile when she should've pressed the button for her security to escort him out—he turned to her. 'You're running out of time. Are you going to waste more by dismissing Valente Ventures' bid without even hearing what I'm proposing?'

Valente Ventures.

The very name screamed predatory capitalism with a capital C. 'Everyone I've met with so far has been a great fit.' On paper at least.

'And yet you've come up short. Zero out of five as of ten minutes ago?'

Another unpleasant jolt careened through her. 'How do you know—?'

'I do my homework, Miss Merchant. And I'm extremely thorough with it.'

'And does that homework include spying on my company?'

He angled his head at her in a way that made her feel…inadequate. A feeling she'd experienced…rarely. And only where it pertained to her relationship with her late parents. She was dealing with that bolt of unnerving surprise when he answered.

'Come on, now, don't be naive. If companies went around wilfully blind to each other's activities, there would be no healthy competition. Besides, didn't I hear you say just now that you've fallen short of your goals?'

Genie pursed her lips, reluctant to hand him the win. 'That still doesn't mean I'm willing to meet with you.'

He watched her with those far too intense eyes for a minute. If he hoped to make her squirm or uncomfortable, he was going to be disappointed. She was used to being an oddity. A creature people whispered about, sometimes within earshot. She'd long since thickened her skin against being distressed by such things.

'You're accustomed to thinking outside the box, are you not?'

'I am but I don't need to with you. You're firmly in the *no* box, Mr Valente.' With a neat pirouette, she turned towards her desk to summon her assistant, and her security, if need be. As she did, she was struck by the odd desire to see this man grapple with her guards, perhaps even best them. He might be adorned with the trappings of power and influence, but she sensed that, underneath it all, Severino Valente could be ruthless when he needed to be. From her recollection of his people, Cardosians were proud and formidable.

And why on earth was she thinking all this?

She reached out her hand to her intercom.

'You want your algorithm to help people. I have a whole country in desperate need of something brave and bold to change their lives. Surely you won't deny them that because the body seeking that help falls under the umbrella of venture capitalist?'

She froze. Turned her head to meet his gaze over her shoulder. 'What people?'

'Mine,' he answered, his tone grave and powerful. 'Cardosia is in the middle of an ecological and economic crisis. The predictive precision of your algorithm for things like weather patterns is nothing short of astounding but I'm sure I don't need to tell you that. It could change the fortunes of an ailing nation. We're not quite teetering on the brink yet but it's only a matter of time. If you think I'm exaggerating, I'm sure you can find out the truth for yourself with a few keystrokes.'

She dropped her hand. She wasn't changing her mind. Not by a long chalk. 'How do I know this isn't a ploy just to get your hands on my intellectual property?

If you've done your homework as you say, then you'll know that two of the entities I met with today outright lied about their true intentions for my algorithm.'

A flash of furious affront whipped across his face and the hairs on her nape stood up. Not because she was afraid of his reaction but because she was riddled with curiosity as to the depths of his passions.

Another hugely troubling first.

She really should've let her business director act on her behalf, saving her from this disturbing interaction. But again Genie felt the oddest sensation in her belly. The one that rejected the idea of missing this… whatever it was.

'I've never needed to lie my way into getting what I want, and I'm not about to start with you. But I'm willing to accommodate a measure of oversight if that will sway to selling your algorithm to me if that's what it takes.'

Oversight.

Maybe he *had* done his homework. Because he was making the very proposal that the previous four candidates had rejected outright. She stepped back from her desk and fully faced him. Only to once again be hit by the veritable force field of his presence.

Had he moved closer?

Because the air was redolent with the scent of sandalwood and spice and warm skin, a curious combination that made her want to take a breath. A *very* deep breath.

'How much oversight?'

'The algorithm will be mine outright and you will not interfere with its day-to-day usage, but I'll allow you a review once every year for the first five years.'

'Just once? A lot can happen in a year, Mr Valente.'

'What I'm offering is more than you received from your other prospective buyers.'

True. And it'd been a concession she was reluctantly willing to negotiate down, as long as she verified beforehand that she was handing her precious property into the right hands. But now he'd opened the prospect of more oversight, it was hard to discard it. Her breath snagged in her midriff when he stepped closer. 'Since I didn't get what I wanted, they too left empty-handed.'

A deep gleam lit his eyes, turning the grey alive and mercurial. 'I'm confident we can both walk away from this with exactly what we want.'

About to respond, she paused when he glanced at his watch.

'Do you have some other pressing matter to attend to?' she snapped, then immediately regretted it. Display of heated emotion was unlike her. Was it because she'd been ready to call this day a loss before this man walked, uninvited, into her office? And now that she'd let herself be intrigued, he was backing away? Was it a tactic?

She met his gaze when he raised his. Again, he studied her for far longer than Genie suspected was polite. She knew because she'd wondered that about herself on a few occasions.

'As a matter of fact, I do,' he responded, his gravel-rough voice causing an unwelcome sensation inside her. 'But I will return this evening. You'll have dinner with me so we can finalise this deal. I'll pick you up at eight.'

The hollow sense of loss when he'd said he was leaving now clashed with the irritating assumption that she would welcome him back or that she would be free to have dinner with him. 'You're getting ahead of youroolf, oir. My time is quite regimented, and it doesn't include—'

'You'd rather go back to the drawing board and attract unsuitable buyers to waste your time than spend a few hours acknowledging that I was the best buyer to start off with?'

His argument was irritatingly logical. But the thought of spending more time with him, with his intuitive eyes fixed on her, made her…unsettled. 'We can have a discussion without the dinner.' Quick. Clinical. *Safe*.

He looked around him, his gaze tracking every sterile surface and impersonal ornament before returning to her. 'I've followed your career. I know there must be a specific reason you wish to let go of your work now. You have a few hours' grace to decide whether you want to sell or not. I suggest you get your people to do their due diligence before this evening. As for the timing, I have dinner reservations I'd rather not go to waste. Unless you have an aversion to eating?'

'I don't,' she snapped. 'But I'm picky about whom I eat with.'

'Then I hope you'll make an exception for a future business acquaintance.' With that he strode towards the door. 'You don't need to leave your cave for longer than three hours,' he mused, the faintest stench of mockery on his face.

Genie was working up a comeback searing enough to make Dr Douglas turn in his grave when Severino Valente paused.

'And, Miss Merchant?'

She contented herself in raising a caustic eyebrow.

His gaze lingered on her face, dropping to her mouth

before rising. 'I meant what I said. I will walk away with what I want. I always do. Nothing else will suffice.'

Genie absently noted that the quivering in her belly had spread all over her body as she watched him saunter through her office door and disappear from view.

She took his advice and pulled up his name the moment she'd changed back into her favourite lounging attire. Although it stuck in her craw the whole time she munched on a carrot while her fingers flew over the keyboard of her beloved supercomputer.

She'd built the first one from scratch when she was eleven and gifted herself the joy of reincarnating one every birthday since she turned sixteen.

While another computer performed a deeper dive, she speed-read through his life.

He was a multibillionaire. *Of course.*

He'd started his venture capitalist outfit at a young age although not as young as she'd been when she'd been forced to survive on her own. But young enough to raise a few eyebrows. Every sign pointed to a superior intellect. One that other notable corporate figures called on for guidance; one that earned him several industry accolades and invitations to keynote positions in conferences where he gave…engrossing speeches.

Genie told herself it was part of her due diligence when she clicked on one of those speeches, only to switch off minutes later when that peculiar tingling sensation returned at the sound of his voice. For whatever reason, Severino Valente's voice caused a distinct reaction in her.

But more and more, she found herself lingering over the details of his personal life. It didn't take much effort to confirm that Seve Valente was also skilled in his pursuit of the opposite sex. Was perhaps even an aficionado. Page after page of his liaisons attested to that, although the man was reportedly very much attached to his *most eligible bachelor* status.

He was healthy. He'd run a few marathons in his younger days.

His blood type wasn't rare enough to be a problem. His family tree was robust enough not to raise any red flags. And he wasn't interested in attaching himself to any particular female.

He's compatible.

Genie wasn't sure when the idea grew from a whisper into a kernel, then into a fertile seed.

Perhaps this—her subconscious working on the problem—was why she'd experienced all that nonsensical tingling and quivering while in his presence.

The reason behind everything she was doing in the first place.

Her next birthday was in ten months. This time she planned on giving herself an altogether different gift.

A life-changing one.

I'm confident we can both walk away from this with exactly what we want.

His words held much more weight now, not that the man knew it himself.

Five minutes of his time; maybe less if her brief previous sexual experience was an indication. That was all she needed.

Provided of course that the remaining digging didn't unearth any nasty surprises.

It didn't. Which was why she stood in another outfit—

one only slightly less comfortable than the last—outside the private entrance to her building at five to eight.

Severino Valente pulled up at eight on the dot in a sleek black sports car, the purr of its engine distinctly electric. If his choice of fuel consumption was designed to impress her, Genie reluctantly admitted it worked.

He stepped out and Genie felt that rush again. It was because of the decision she'd made, she told herself. Nothing else.

That assurance gave her permission to watch him approach. He'd changed too, swapped his formal shirt for a black one, open at the neck minus a tie, over which he wore another bespoke but more casual jacket coupled with matching trousers. His hair looked a little windswept but it was his face that arrested her scrutiny.

Grey eyes watched with impossibly more intensity before swinging past to the two burly guards positioned a few feet away.

'Dismiss your bodyguards. You won't need them tonight.'

Genie started, then berated herself for her lapse in concentration. She opened her mouth to do as he bade, but held her tongue for several seconds. Dr Douglas would perhaps describe it as childish but she didn't want to show this man how eagerly her senses jumped to accommodate him. Without her express permission.

When he raised that sardonic eyebrow, she turned and nodded her dismissal.

She followed him to the passenger side of his car, where he hesitated before opening the door, his gaze tracking her body shamelessly from head to toe.

'After the way we parted, I was convinced you'd come out in a tracksuit. You look stunning, Genie.'

The whirlpool in her belly spun faster. 'This isn't a social outing, Mr Valente. You don't need to fall into predictable platitudes.'

One corner of his mouth lifted. 'I don't think you want me to stray outside predictability, Genie. Otherwise, I risk being intensely inappropriate.'

Sensation akin to mild electricity flowed through her veins as his gaze lingered on her mouth. To combat it, she grasped at the first defensive straw. 'If you're thinking of making juvenile rubbing lamp or wish jokes about my name, don't bother. I've heard them all.'

He pulled the door open with smooth, suppressed force. Waited until she was installed in the bucket seat before shutting the door.

She watched him round the low bonnet of the car, his leonine glide impossible to resist watching. When an oncoming set of headlights lit up his face, the static intensified.

She continued to watch him once he slid in beside her. And then even as he reached across and secured her seat belt, reminding her that she'd forgotten. Reminding her of his focus-altering scent when she inhaled.

'I'm many things, Genie. Juvenile isn't one of them.'

She believed him. From what she'd learned of him, he'd vaulted from pre-puberty straight into adulthood. Her search for those few vital adolescent years had come up empty in the time she'd had. As much as she didn't want to be, she was intrigued by those missing years.

'And it's okay to admit you find me attractive, too,' he added as he slid the car into gear and accelerated from her sanctuary.

Genie shrugged, eagerly falling back on firm and

solid logic. 'It's a physiological reaction to the opposite sex. I'm confident I could line up fifty men on the street right now and guarantee I will have a similar reaction to at least two of them.'

From the dashboard lights she caught something distinctly...primitive flash in his eyes. 'You're sure about that?'

The tingling in her body escalated and that scent seemed to reach out to her, demanding that she breathe it...*him*...in... 'Oh, yes. The very structure of our society has primed us to find more than one individual compatible enough to have sex with. Otherwise there wouldn't be almost eight billion of us walking the earth.' She tilted her head, allowed her gaze to trail him up and down. 'Surely an exemplary specimen such as yourself wouldn't conform to the archaic thinking that there is only one person for every human being on the planet? The proverbial soulmate?'

His nostrils flared, as if she'd touched a nerve.

Don't pick on the weak.

She pursed her lips and gave it few moments' thought. Was she stepping out of line? She didn't think so.

She'd weighed up her opponent before embarking on this skirmish and she was sure—hell, she was confident—he had the mental dexterity to keep up with her.

'For their sake, I'd advise you not to summon those fifty men in my presence. I won't be responsible for my actions otherwise.' There was a scalpel-sharp edge to his tone. A tightening of his grip around the steering wheel.

She frowned. 'You're...not pleased with my response.'

A short laugh grated from his throat. 'I will let it slide just this once, *pequeña*,' he rumbled.

His clenched jaw suggested the proposed 'slide' wasn't an immediate thing, so Genie chose to remain silent for the rest of the short journey.

Silence continued to reign as they were seated in a private booth in a secluded part of the Mayfair restaurant that boasted three Michelin stars on a discreet plaque at the door.

But after he'd ordered wine and their first course had been delivered, she clasped her hands on the pristine napkin in her lap.

Time to lay a card or two on the table.

'I struggle with social cues. You should know that.'

He looked up from his veal starter and fixed his eyes on her. Silence thudded between them for a long stretch. 'Most geniuses do,' he responded eventually.

There was that peculiar fluttering in her stomach again. She looked down at her scallops.

Maybe she should've stayed away from the molluscs. But…she'd never had an adverse effect from eating them before. Therefore the logical conclusion was that something else…or *someone* else was responsible for the sensation.

She looked up.

He was watching her with those leonine eyes. Was she expected to thank him? Was his response courteous or merely observatory?

Several minutes passed before she realised they were staring at one another. That his mouth, while unmoving, held the minutest hint of amusement.

'Is something wrong with your food?'

'I haven't decided yet.'

'Explain.'

Her grip tightened momentarily on her fork. 'There's a sensation in my stomach that I can't apply a source to. Well, no, that's not true. I mean, I'm not sure if it's indigestion or...'

'Or?'

Mild shock waves rippled through her. 'I don't think I have a precise name for it.'

This time his lips developed a distinct curve. A smile. A...transformative smile that held her attention completely. She'd known that he was a handsome man. But she hadn't taken into account just how compelling a simple smile could be. How...*enrapturing.*

Then she frowned. Because that smile looked entirely at her expense. 'Am I missing something, Mr Valente?'

'I dare say you are, *pequeña,*' he said cryptically.

Which rattled her cage even further. 'I don't like mysteries.'

'You don't? Isn't chasing mystery what fuels your work?'

She shook her head. 'You're confusing drive with mysterious.'

'At the risk of sounding simplistic, your brain has informed you that you're attracted to me. Your body is merely catching up.'

She blinked. 'By giving me indigestion?'

'When you get used to it, you'll be able to differentiate it from indigestion.'

'You're assuming that this feeling will last longer than I wish it to.'

'While it's your choice whether to act on it or not,

some things are beyond your body's control. This is one of them.'

'I disagree,' she snapped immediately. This felt like something she needed to defend herself from.

This time the movement of his lips was more pronounced, redirecting her attention from his eyes to his mouth. To the near perfect symmetry of the thinner upper and the fuller bottom. To the divot dissecting the top lip in a riveting V-shape and—

'First lesson in this new realm you find yourself in, Genie. Don't stare at a man's mouth like that unless you wish to provoke a specific reaction.'

'What sort of reaction?'

A sound emitted from his throat, one she couldn't quite decipher immediately because it was animalistic in nature. 'That of the carnal kind. You stare at my mouth and all I can think about is how much I want to taste yours.'

A pulse of heat surged from the very place she was experiencing the sensation. No, not quite accurate. It was lower. In her pelvis. Between her thighs. She crossed her legs but the hot tingle didn't dissipate. So she dragged her gaze upward. But then she was confronted with eyes that didn't look quite the same as they had a few moments ago. They were heated, narrowed. Laser focused on her in a way that made her thighs clench tighter.

'Understood. I will endeavour to not stare at your mouth, Mr Valente.'

Another sound surged from his throat again, more animalistic than before. It sounded like…a growl. It was primitive enough to make her grimace inwardly. But not enough to stop another intensely physical reaction.

Wetness between her legs.

Stiffening and pinching of her nipples.

Slow drag of heat through her pelvis.

Reactions of the carnal kind.

Inconvenient while it lasted but perhaps advantageous where it counted.

Setting her fork down, she linked her fingers once more. 'I've come to a decision, Mr Valente.'

That fierce light she was beginning to attribute to heightened emotion lit his eyes before he penned it once more. 'I'm eager to hear it.'

Unexpected emotion clogged her throat, demanding she clear it before she could speak. It was perfectly rational. This was everything she'd been working towards. A lifelong wish guarded and nurtured through her solitary and neglected childhood. It was right she gave it due gravity.

So she took another breath. 'I'll consider selling you my algorithm on one condition.'

'Which is?' he prodded.

'Which is that you impregnate me.'

CHAPTER TWO

SEVE HAD CHOSEN this restaurant for its privacy, pleasing ambience and excellent cuisine.

He'd spotted a few business acquaintances on his way to their table but the ultimate reason he'd wanted to come here was because discretion was guaranteed.

There were no raucous birthday celebrations or hen dos deafening everyone else.

Which was why he *knew* he hadn't misheard her.

So it was most likely the shock that made him demand, 'What did you say?' in tones that sounded like the crunch of broken glass.

The stunning genius in front of him merely pursed her lips, immediately drawing his attention—as had happened aggravatingly often since they'd first met this afternoon—to plump crimson lips that stood out like a neon sign on her otherwise pale face. Coupled with her astonishing green eyes fringed by thick black lashes, they made her face resemble a fairy-tale character come to life.

It was the first of many revelatory shocks when he'd impelled his way into her office this morning. Before then, he'd only seen grainy pictures of the child prodigy turned innovative genius who'd written the unparalleled ground-breaking code with the ability to significantly combat the global climate crisis, amongst many things.

Nowhere on that list of astounding revelations had he anticipated…*this* reality.

I struggle with social cues.

Abrupt but vulnerable. Honest. A brief glimpse behind her impressive titanium armour.

Dios mio. How on earth could five random words immediately give him a hard-on? Five words that should make him hurry up and be done with this so he could get on with the important business of helping Cardosia, but instead made him want to know everything about her. Like how she'd even arrived at her absurd demand.

She'd floored him completely—a feat most would pay hard-earned money to witness when it came to Seve Valente.

'Ideally, I'd like it to happen before our deal is concluded. I wish to give birth before my twenty-ninth birthday. If it helps, my ovulation window is from next Wednesday to Saturday.'

Seve was glad he hadn't taken a bite of food. He feared he would be writhing on the floor choking on his veal by now.

'Eugenie.'

She froze, her green eyes widening to saucers. 'You know my given name,' she muttered before she shook her head. 'Of course you do. If it helps progress things, I'll allow you to call me that. No one else does though.'

'Why not?'

She blinked. Then a tiny spark he hadn't even been aware of died in her eyes. Immediately, illogically, he wanted it back. 'My parents forbade anyone from calling me that. They said Genie was more appropriate. Because it sounded a lot like—'

'Genius?' he guessed.

Another spark died and he bit back a growl.

'Yes.'

He inhaled long and deep to establish some semblance of calm. 'When we're more…comfortable with each other you'll tell me which one you prefer. For now you'll repeat what you just said about…wanting a…' He paused, not sure why he couldn't even utter the word.

She couldn't know that on his list of things he intended to avoid in this life was fathering a child. That the still vivid horror of his own childhood demanded that the label never be pinned on him.

'A child, Mr Valente. I want you to provide me with the requisite equipment to create a baby.'

The requisite equipment…

Was it possible to be punch-drunk having consumed only a few drops of alcohol? He had to give her her due, though. It wasn't often he was this astounded by anything any more.

At the ripe old age of thirty-six he was severely jaded. Nothing and no one had surprised him for a long time. People were predictably greedy, cruel and selfish, and not necessarily in that order.

On paper, Genie Merchant had been just another run-of-the-mill eccentric genius who smugly believed that the world revolved around her. He'd encountered more than his fair share in his line of business. They often laboured under the wrong belief that their wish should be everyone else's command and when they discovered that Severino Valente didn't intend to jump, they tended to throw a strop, then postured before quickly capitulating to his will.

He'd waited for *weeks* for Genie Merchant to fall into line. Had watched her attempt to align herself with a trove of unsuitable candidates. Hell, he'd had to slyly step in once or twice to ensure the more deplorable runners on her list didn't progress past the initial consideration stage.

After weeks had gone by, and after he'd had to admit that this time *he* was the one destined to capitulate, it'd chafed for a while before he'd set the unfamiliar feeling aside for the greater good.

For Cardosia.

'I'm a man who's unequivocal about stating what he wants. And yet I'm under the impression that I've skipped several rungs of this conversation without due process.'

A pink tongue slicked over her Snow White lips as she shook her head. 'You're not. You haven't. I'm also a woman who doesn't hold back from stating what she wants. I've told you what I want. Mindless chitchat isn't necessary.'

Slowly, an unnerving sensation wound its way like a dark underground river through him. 'Tell me you didn't make this proposal to anyone else. Is this a contingency that was attached to all your meetings today?' Why did that matter? And, *Dios mio*, why did the very idea of it fill him with such fury?

True, he hadn't expected the near-reclusive genius to be so intensely…feminine. Alluring and breathtakingly beautiful. Not the gangly teenager wearing regulation nerdy glasses with mousy dark hair, oftentimes hiding behind her more publicity-seeking parents.

The reality of her had been so shocking that, for several seconds, he'd believed he'd walked into the wrong office.

No one had warned him the genius with the jaw-dropping IQ inhabited the body of a nineteen-fifties pin-up. That the ropey, lifeless hair was in fact lustrous tresses that invited a man…*him*…to sink his fingers into the heavy mass, grip it firmly to nudge her head back so he could plunder those sinful lips. To learn her taste and savour her essence.

And yes, his initial reaction after seeing her in the flesh for the first time had been…visceral. He was a red-blooded male with vigorous passions and a healthy libido, after all. But—

'I did not,' she replied crisply.

A layer of that furore subsided at her answer, but he still remained highly out of sorts, a baffling and irritating condition.

All he had to do was utter the *no* lodged like a heavy stone in his gut. Redirect the conversation back to the pertinent and pressing reason they were here. And yet all he could think of was that once he denied her with that 'no', she would seek the next candidate. That *he* would be consigned to the reject list.

So what?

He didn't want children. Definitely not for the sake of procreating to fulfil the cachet objective the way his parents had. And most definitely not as a manipulation tool or a bargaining chip to be peddled for power. His whole childhood had been a joke, a cruel game of false affection, abject neglect and quid pro quo no child should be subjected to.

It was an experience that had, if not damaged him, at

least psychologically scarred him. The risk that he could pass it on to his child, that he might unconsciously visit that same cruelty on an innocent offspring?

No. *Never.*

The searing reminder burned away the peculiar sensation swimming in his gut, attempting to move that stone. And when he exhaled next, it was with the reassurance that common sense had reasserted itself. 'The answer is no, Miss Merchant.'

Her shoulders stiffened for a fraction of time, then deflated a little. Before she gave a curt, dismissive nod. 'Very well.'

His eyes narrowed and that furore returned, twice as incendiary. '*Very well?* What does that mean?' The intensity of his reaction shocked Seve.

As it did Genie, if her sharp intake of breath was an indication. For several seconds, she merely blinked at him. Then, she reached for her glass, taking a sip of water and setting it down in precise motions before she glanced at him. 'I sense that I'm supposed to either beg, convince you to change your mind or take your answer at face value. Option number three seems the most logical. We're both pressed for time, and you stated a few minutes ago that you're an unequivocal man so it stands to reason that you wouldn't say no just to play games with me.'

Seve was…nonplussed. And he hated it. This woman was drawing emotions from him he deeply resented.

Then get back on course. Be done with this.

He forced a reluctant nod. 'Good. This dinner is to discuss you selling your algorithm to me. You haven't lost sight of that, I hope?'

Her lashes swept down for a moment but when she

lifted her head again only the faintest shadow in her eyes reflected the peculiar conversation that had just taken place. 'No, I haven't.'

A growl rose in his throat, but he quickly killed it. 'You're not what I expected.'

'I've heard that often enough before, Mr Valente.'

'Seve.'

'Excuse me?'

'Call me Seve.'

The pulse leapt faster at her throat and his fingers itched to trace it. 'I would rather not.'

'Why do you want a child?' *Dios*, why was he pursuing this?

She stiffened, then waved an elegant hand. 'That's none of your business. You refused my request. I don't owe you an explanation.'

His insides clenched. It was the same sort of dismissiveness he'd been subjected to as a child. The sort of treatment he'd tried—and succeeded— in throwing into a vault and tossing away the key. Now that unpleasant box was rattling, threatening to fly open and throw up all his bitterness and resentment about his childhood.

Only if you allow it. Only if you dwell on this.

Deeming him dismissed, she started to quiz him about his plans for her algorithm.

The subject was close enough to his heart that he could rattle away answers without guise or reservation. Her algorithm would direct the scientists and environmentalists where to focus their energy in reversing the ecological damage being done to Cardosia. Amongst many other advantages. But even as he rattled off his country's many needs, his unanswered questions loomed larger as they ate their main course, then the dessert Genie ordered and the espresso he chose for himself.

By the time she sank her silver spoon into the strawberry and cream concoction and lifted it to her mouth, Seve couldn't hold back any longer.

'You're going to sell to me. We both know that.'

Her green eyes sparked and something ignited within him. 'I wouldn't be so presump—'

He held up a halting hand. 'If this was going nowhere you wouldn't have ordered dessert.'

She looked down at the concoction as if surprised it was in front of her. 'Perhaps I have a near-addictive sweet tooth that needs servicing.'

'Which you can indulge in the privacy of your home once you get there. You're not that undisciplined.' She opened her mouth again but he beat her to it once more. 'This is a social cue I can help you out with, Miss Merchant. You're lingering because you're not ready for this dinner to end. You've done your homework on me, and it was more than satisfactory because you would've cancelled if you had deep enough reservations. Don't forget, I know you threw Frank Graham out within five minutes. You know I'm the most viable candidate. So it begs the question, why are you holding back from giving us both what we want?'

She set her spoon down and folded her hands in her lap. Seve was beginning to recognise that cue, too. She did it to guard herself from the gravity of her needs. To collect herself before she gave too much away.

It stood to reason that a woman with her level of intelligence would need to, otherwise she would be taken advantage of. And why did that *too* send a pulse of fury through him?

Perhaps he needed his own head examined.

'This is my life's work thus far. It's logical that I give it more than a meal's duration worth of consideration, don't you think?'

Something snagged in his chest, but he dismissed it. He was done with entertaining peculiar feelings. 'Yes, it is. And while you do I have questions of my own.'

Shock, then wariness filmed her eyes. 'You do?'

He shrugged. 'I have some burden of responsibility too. One of which is to know why a young woman like you is eager to offload her life's work. And before you say it's none of my business, I must insist that your answer is contingent on whether this deal goes forward, of course.'

'Why?'

'Because I'd be a fool to go in blind only for you to turn around and build a similar code a year from now and sell it to my competitor.'

Affront quickened her breath, causing her breasts to strain against her dress. It was enough to flood him with red-hot desire. Enough to thicken his shaft and trigger potent craving he hadn't experienced in a long time.

'I would never do that.'

'I haven't got this far in life by taking people at their word, Miss Merchant. I'm sensing you have experience of the same.'

She swallowed and, again, he couldn't stop himself from following the graceful line of her throat, wondering how that curve in her neck would feel beneath his lips. On his tongue. Her scent filling his nostrils.

Por l'amor de…

'I can put that in writing if you want.'

They both held still.

Because, in that moment, the gravity of her words, her capitulation, needed its presence acknowledged.

After a full minute, she exhaled, her shoulders relaxing a fraction. She looked away momentarily before her bold gaze met his again.

Still, she said nothing.

He hid a smile. She was formidable. Enough to tweak and hold his interest. It made him wonder in what other ways she could achieve that. And he silently shook his head.

Theirs *should* and would remain a transactional relationship. He didn't have the head space to deal with the untamed emotions she triggered in him.

'You will sell me your code.' He needed the words spoken out loud so he could finish this and move on to more important things. Like helping his people. Like stopping his uncle from stripping his beloved homeland of every last resource.

'Yes.'

The affirmative answer he'd wished. And yet…

Suddenly, he wanted to be somewhere else. Somewhere the presence of others didn't intrude on this moment.

'We'll take your dessert to go,' he said, shocking himself once more. Hadn't he promised himself one minute ago that he'd move on?

'Go where?'

Our separate ways. Now that I have what I want.

'Somewhere quieter where we won't be interrupted. The English weather is being uncharacteristically cooperative. Inside or outside. We can go anywhere you want.'

Her nose wrinkled cutely. 'I'm not an outside type of person.'

He shrugged. 'Because you haven't been exposed to the *right* type of outside.'

'I'm not sure what that means.'

He fished out his wallet and tossed a few hundred pounds on the table. Summoning the waiter, he gave his request.

A minute later, her dessert was boxed up and the *maître d'* was wishing them a good evening.

But when they stepped outside, a spurt of misgiving sprang up.

He'd never mixed business with pleasure and he was certain he wasn't about to start. But almost instantly, he was flooded by the unsettling sensations that had been driving him all night.

Seve wasn't a man who liked to admit weakness, but as he sped through the streets of London towards his destination, he couldn't fail to register that he was helpless against the compulsion pounding in his veins.

Compulsion that had nothing to do with the fact that he now had within his grasp his most effective tool of toppling his uncle's power and setting Cardosia back on the right track.

And everything to do with Genie Merchant.

Somehow he wasn't entirely surprised when he pulled up to his private parking space in the underground garage of his duplex.

'Where are we?' Genie asked.

She'd remained silent throughout the journey. Now she looked around for a moment before turning her gaze to him with one eyebrow raised.

'Somewhere you can finish that—' he nodded at the box in her hand '—while we finalise the terms of sale.'

Her fingers spasmed on the box, a tiny betraying movement he caught nonetheless. Because everything about her interested him to the point of slavish intrigue.

He realised he'd held his breath when it rushed out at her eventual nod of consent. He unfastened her seat belt with more alacrity than he'd intended, and with every click of their footsteps towards the private elevator that shot them up to his penthouse, he ignored the inner voice demanding to know what he was doing.

The East London residence he used when he was in England had been constructed to impress men of his business stature and influence. Every sophisticated amenity was within reach. But what had sold the vast, luxurious space to Seve—as was the intention—was the view both day and night.

At almost eleven p.m., the carpet of lights and distinct icons of the bridges that dissected the Thames drew Genie past the soft dove-grey walls interspersed with some of his favourite art and sculptures, past the sumptuous matching sofas and lofty ceilings, past the Italian marble floors and the specially commissioned Swarovski crystal chandeliers.

To the outside.

He watched her make a beeline for the wide outdoor sofa facing the spectacular view, something inside kicking wildly as he witnessed her unfettered interest in *his* view. He hid a smile as she took it all in.

Then, he went indoors to his kitchen, returning with a silver spoon, which he held out to her.

She looked up, a touch surprised. 'Oh. Thanks.'

Her thumb brushed over his knuckles as she took the utensil from him. Her breathing faltered, a tinge of colour staining her cheeks at his unabashed interest.

Again, he tried to smother his wild senses when her gaze swept down, depriving him of the vital connection.

Stepping around the sofa, he took the opposite end, and watched as she ate her sweet.

Two bites in, Seve crossed his legs to hide the effect of what the spoon continually disappearing into her mouth did to his libido.

Dios mio. Perhaps it was time to call up a past flame, take care of his physical need with a night of vigorous sex so he could think more clearly.

His last visit to Cardosia four months ago had driven home the urgency of his actions, and left room for little else. But now he had a solution within reach he couldn't be distracted by—

'Six months.'

Although he knew what she was referring to, he still raised his eyebrows. He told himself he wanted to make sure they were on the same page, but underneath that prompt, there was a burning need to hear her voice. To keep her engaged. 'Six months?' he echoed.

Her green gaze flitted over to him, then rushed over his body before returning to the view. But he hadn't missed her quickened breath when she glanced at his torso and crossed legs. She took her time to swallow before she spoke.

'The oversight period. I want to review it every six months.'

He shook his head. 'Fifteen months.'

Her eyes returned to his filled with more fire. 'No. Ten months. That's six times over the course of five years. That's non-negotiable.'

He would see this intriguing creature every ten months. Possibly pick her incredible brain on ways to better improve the dire conditions in Cardosia. Keep the lines of communication open.

It was a sensible option he would be a fool to dismiss.

Are you sure that's all it is?

He gritted his teeth, intensely irritated with the unrelenting inner voice. 'I will agree to ten months, as long as it's done on site.'

Her spoon, holding another delicate concoction, paused halfway to her mouth as she considered his addendum. It shouldn't have been sexy. He didn't have a sweet tooth in his body, and yet he found himself leaning forward, swiping a crumb off the corner of her fork with his thumb and tasting it. 'Just so we're clear, that means I want you in Cardosia. In person. No exceptions.'

Her hand trembled a little, her eyelashes fluttering as she raised the morsel and closed her plumps lips over it. By the time her tongue flicked out, Seve was fully erect, the pressure in his groin unbearable and every square inch of his body on fire.

God, he needed to get laid. Like yesterday.

Again, she chewed and swallowed before she answered, keeping them both waiting. 'I can do that. Cardosia is in a beautiful part of the world.'

Pride and determination burst to life in his chest. '*Sí.* I intend to do everything in my power to ensure it stays that way.' From afar, though. Returning home roused his demons to life.

Seve knew that was the moment he had her total agreement. It was also probably when he should've ended their meeting. Driven her home or, better yet, called his twenty-four-hour car service and placed some vitally prudent distance between them.

Instead, he pulled out his phone and dialled a familiar number. He finished the five-minute conversation to find her staring at him.

'You're getting the contract documents drawn up right now? It's almost midnight,' she stated in surprise.

'I have lawyers on retainer in several time zones in the world. My New York lawyers are standing by to get started.' He paused, his gaze drifting over her face with a hunger he was unaccustomed to. 'Do you wish to get the ball rolling or do you need to get your beauty sleep?'

Her chin went up, mild outrage in her eyes. 'Don't pigeonhole me with stereotypes, Mr Valente. Do *you* require beauty sleep?'

The way his senses were rampaging, sleep was the last thing on his mind right now. 'Not at all, *pequeña*,' he murmured. 'I can go all night.'

He stifled a groan as colour rushed freely and enthusiastically up her neck and into her cheeks. He clenched his fist tighter, fighting the need to stroke her skin, feel that gush with his fingers. 'So can I,' she tossed out in a defiant, breathlessly husky voice.

Seve dragged a hand through his hair, sadistically tugging on the strands to better concentrate his mind. The sexual chemistry between them was insane but Cardosia was more important.

'Good.' He sent a quick text before putting his phone away. 'Then let's talk numbers. I know your highest bid was eight hundred million. I'm prepared to top that to one billion dollars if you throw in your building and all relevant staff as part of the deal. I need your tech experts to configure the algorithm to suit my needs as soon as possible.'

Her jaw sagged, her luscious lips dropping open as she inhaled in shock. 'I... A billion dollars?'

'Yes. That's how badly I want you— Your algorithm.' He allowed himself a smile. 'And it's not without pleasure for me to welcome another woman to the billion-dollar club.'

'I don't care about that,' she stated primly, her eyes flashing again.

He believed her. He'd studied her long enough to know money wasn't what drove her.

So what did?

Unbidden, his gaze dropped to her flat stomach. The belly she intended to fill with a baby as soon as possible if her statement at dinner was an indication. With a billion dollars she'd never have to work another day in her life. She would be free to have an entire brood if she wanted.

Without him...

'What do you care about, then?' he asked before he could stop himself.

She started, her attention drawn from the stratospheric figure he'd tossed into her lap to his question.

'I thought we agreed to leave personal business alone?'

'Did we? I don't recall agreeing to anything of the sort. You said it wasn't my business.'

'It still isn't—'

She paused when she saw movement behind them.

The text he'd sent was to the twenty-four-hour concierge service. The attendant wheeled in a sterling silver tray with glasses and a bottle of vintage Dom Perignon set in an ice bucket.

Seve directed him where to put it then nodded his

thanks. Once they were alone, he popped the champagne, poured her a glass and took one for himself before he sat back.

'What shall we drink to, besides the obvious?'

Her nostrils fluttered. 'You're determined. But you must know this isn't going anywhere because I'm equally determined.'

'Think of it less as prying and more like…humouring me.' It was a deeper, more visceral need than that, once whose source he couldn't quite fathom.

Or could he?

While, on the surface, Genic Merchant had exemplary qualities stemming from her brilliant mind, she was the last person he would've laid a maternal label on. Which was why her demand had knocked him sideways. But it had done more than that.

It'd unearthed unwanted memories of his childhood, and the reasons why he didn't want children. And, perhaps equally importantly, why not everyone who wanted to procreate should.

His own parents were a typical example.

While his childhood had been hellish, not once had he wished for a sibling to alleviate that loneliness. Because even as a small child the last thing he'd wanted was for a brother, even worse, a sister to suffer the way he had. To live in fear of the wrong word or look inviting corporal punishment, which was gleefully doled out under 'character building'.

It would've been unbearable to watch another child sentenced to his father's and uncle's brutal fists at the smallest infraction. Even worse to see his mother do nothing while her son was abused.

It was a small crumb of comfort in a hellscape he'd

thought he'd put behind him until Genie Merchant unearthed the memories.

'Maybe I want the same thing you claim you do. To leave the world a better place than I found it,' she said, blithely unaware of the churning within him.

'By filling it with babies?' he gritted out with more bitterness than he'd intended to reveal.

She stiffened, her skin going pale as she stared at him with pained eyes.

A flash of regret fired through him but it wasn't deep enough for him to issue an apology. Because he felt strongly about this. Perhaps too strongly.

'I think we should stick to business from here on out, Mr Valente,' she said stiffly.

But the boy turned man who wore the scarred consequences, and understood what an ill-thought-out plan to procreate for the hell of it could produce, wasn't ready to let this go.

'So you can get to the more urgent business of asking another man to give you a child?' Again, his whole being reacted violently to Genie Merchant repeating her request to some other man. To offering her body to another to take, to touch. To fill with his seed.

With a barely stifled snarl, he launched to his feet, the untouched champagne spilling over his fingers as he stalked to the low glass wall bordering the terrace. He wasn't even aware he was growling until she cleared her throat behind him.

'I believe your social cues are abandoning you, Mr Valente.' The sharp click of her setting down her glass on the coffee table made him turn around. 'Perhaps we should take this back up in the morn—'

'No!' Her eyes widened at his tone, and he forced

himself to inhale slowly. 'No,' He modulated his voice. 'Consider the matter dropped.' *For now.* It wasn't… shouldn't concern him what she did with her new-found wealth. Or her body.

She tilted her head, studying him like a new strain of code she found interesting. When his body started to react to that too, he surged forward.

'The subject of children… unsettles you,' she murmured, open curiosity stamped on her face.

He clenched his teeth. 'The frivolity with which people pursue parenthood does, yes.'

Her eyes shadowed and, after a moment, she looked past him to the view. 'I'm not a frivolous person, Mr Valente.'

'Seve.'

Her gaze swung back to him. 'What?'

'Another request for you to call me Seve,' he pressed with biting insistence alarming in its intensity.

She blinked. 'Why?' The question was filled with genuine curiosity. And burgeoning self-awareness that flared renewed heat in her cheeks.

'Because it will please me.'

Her breath feathered out in a little rush. 'Why would I want to please you?'

He shrugged. 'Call it an experiment. Do it and see the result.'

She frowned. 'Why—?'

'Don't overthink it, Genie.'

'I rarely overthink. I give every matter an allotted amount of time. Then I move on.'

His lips twitched and once again he acknowledged how much he enjoyed their verbal jousting. It was almost enough to soothe his ruffled nerves. *Almost.*

'That's not true, is it? You were dwelling on your disappointment when I came to your office this morning.'

Her throat moved and he vaguely registered that she was nervous. 'You're mistaken, I'm sure.'

He stared down into the bubbles in his drink for several moments. 'Let's make each other a promise. Let's always be honest with each other.'

She considered it, her gaze once again flitting to the view before meeting his. 'That's acceptable.'

'That's acceptable, what?' he enquired mildly, his tone at variance with the jangling nerves performing acrobatics within him. This was yet another absurdity he couldn't figure out. And yet the compulsion raged without cease.

Her nostrils fluttered and for the longest second, he thought she would refuse. And then, 'That's acceptable, *Seve.*'

Perhaps the fates knew why he'd insisted. Because something clenched decadently inside him when she uttered his name. When she tilted her head, exposing the sleek, graceful line of her neck and asked, 'Did I say it right?'

'You know you did,' he responded thickly. 'Your perfectionism won't let you get it wrong. Say it again,' he commanded, pretty sure he was skirting some dangerous line but not caring in that moment.

'Seve,' she whispered, unconsciously sultry in a way that he suspected she wasn't aware of, which made it all the more desirable.

'Dios mío. Qué demonios está pasando?' he muttered, half expecting his inner voice would mock him for asking what the hell was going on.

'*Dígame usted,*' she replied in perfect Spanish. *You tell me.*

His head reared up. 'I forgot you speak my language.'

'And several others besides,' she reminded him without fanfare.

Witnessing her being so comfortable in her utter brilliance? It was irresistible.

But there was one language she was untutored in. She couldn't quite hide her arousal.

Her body all but *trembled* as she stared at his mouth then his body with blatant hunger that only fuelled his own. That chipped away at his already failing resistance.

'We seem to have lost sight of our toast.'

'Nothing has followed a predictable pattern this evening,' she answered, picking up her glass.

He clinked his glass to hers, took a healthy gulp of vintage champagne, then uttered more wildly unpredicted words. 'Maybe it's a sign to just go with the flow.'

She sipped her champagne, then shook her head, bewilderment mingling with her arousal. 'But…why can't I resist this…pull? It's quite infuriating, but I can't stop.'

Seve groaned. With every cell in his body he wished she hadn't uttered those words. Hadn't been unabashed about what she was feeling.

Because the next flood that surged washed away the last of his resistance. Made him set his glass aside and spear his fingers through her hair the way he'd been fantasising about all evening. Hell, all damn day!

And heaven help him if the strands weren't as silky and luxurious as he'd imagined. She didn't pull away.

Dios, she stared at him with such unfettered and curious desire, he wondered how innocent she was. Whether she knew what such a look did to a man.

Leaning down, he gave into the urge and brushed his lips across hers, featherlight and flame-stoking. 'Does that pull hunger for this?' he breathed against her satin-soft mouth.

She swayed closer. 'Yes.'

'And this?' He nipped at the corner of her mouth.

She gasped and her eyes fluttered closed, her body surging closer. 'Yes.'

Seve licked the sting he'd caused, then continued licking until her lips parted for him. But before he could delve in to devour the way his senses screamed at him to, a splash of cold wetness stopped him.

They both looked down to see her champagne spilling over her fingers.

Seve relieved her of the glass, then, capturing her fingers, he drew them to his mouth, licking the tart liquid from them. And with each lap of her smooth skin, the blood pounded harder through his veins, her hitched moans lighting further flames to his senses.

'How infuriated are you right now, Genie?' he mocked teasingly.

'Extremely,' she returned huskily, her beautiful eyes limpid with desire, her breath emerging in pants. 'But please don't stop.'

Lust raged free, the restraint he'd placed on himself all night unshackled. He sucked on her fingers until her knees gave way.

He caught her in his arms, sealed his mouth to hers and finally delivered the kiss they both craved.

Then because he knew in his bones it wouldn't be enough, that nothing but complete possession would do, Seve swung her into his arms, turned and strode purposefully indoors.

CHAPTER THREE

SHE WASN'T DRUNK, at least not from alcohol. She'd only taken a sip of champagne and spilled a significant portion of the rest.

Yet, her senses were in free fall, floating through sensation she'd never experienced before. All created by the man she'd agreed to sell her life's work to.

The man who'd refused her brazen request and should therefore be on her *strictly platonic* list. The man who had arrogantly spelled out her attraction to him and should therefore be on her *thinks too insufferably highly of himself so stay away* list.

And yet he was the same man her body strained against, the one around whose neck she tightened her arms as he walked them towards goodness knew where. Whose eyes devoured her like a raging forest fire without mercy. Who made every cell in her body tingle although even she knew that was scientifically unlikely.

The spaces he walked through were lit by low lamps that gave her brief glimpses of impeccable taste and decor. And even if they were fully lit, she wouldn't have taken proper note.

Because the drugging effect of his lips on her neck made her eyes too heavy to keep open, every self-preserving instinct paused while she drifted through nirvana.

But when he reached his destination and set her down, she roused long enough to note they were in a vast, supremely masculine bedroom, the greys and whites and chrome from before echoed throughout the space.

And then Seve was commanding her attention again, sensual promise in the hands that drew her to his body, in the fingers that spiked back into her hair, and in the lips descending on hers.

A fleeting thought *un*-paused her consciousness for the briefest moment.

Was she really doing this? Agitating an already un-settling evening with sexual chemistry?

Yes.

A brush of his firm lips on hers. 'These lips have driven me crazy all day.'

Genie hung onto her cogency long enough to chal-lenge him. Because she'd learned something new this evening. She *enjoyed* sparring intellectually with him. 'Why? Because you don't like what they had to say?'

He laughed, and the sound filled her with even more impossible yearning. 'On the contrary. I relished every word because they intrigued me. Far too much. They also made me want to do more of this.'

He swooped down and recaptured her lips, stoking the fervour already churning in her midriff. She'd had minimal health issues in her life, but Genie recalled one particularly virulent fever she'd had one winter. This sensation was like that but in a much more *excit-ing* way. A way that made her crave more of it. Made her want to burn with it. Because every logical deduction promised an explosive outcome.

And she so wanted to explode.

'More,' she gasped when he lifted his head.

He didn't deliver. Instead his eyes narrowed, his blazing gaze promising things she couldn't quite fathom but actively craved. 'Beg me,' he commanded gruffly. 'Beg me for what you want, Genie.'

It should've been nonsensical. Illogical.

He was denying them both what they plainly wanted. She wasn't delusional enough to have conjured up the need she saw stamped boldly on his face. And yet he was asking her to degrade herself. To lower herself...

So why did she want to?

Why did the very thought of it send further flames leaping through her bloodstream, intensifying the chemical reaction to this man?

A slow, conceited smile spread over his lips. Lips reddened and slightly swollen from devouring hers. 'The idea turns you on, doesn't it?'

Self-preservation dictated she deny it, but she hesitated.

Let's always be honest with each other.

'Why does it?' she asked instead.

'Because your instincts tell you it will heighten your experience. Both our experiences. You yearn to say it. I need to hear it. Sometimes it's as simple as that.'

Was it?

She'd never begged for anything in her life. Not even the affection and regard her parents had cruelly denied her. Despite it being the hardest thing she'd ever done, she'd smothered those impulses until they were buried deep. Not deep enough to rescue her from the pain of their actions but enough so no one could guess her torment. Her abject loneliness.

Would it have been as simple as voicing the words? Pleading for what she wanted?

Or was she slapping a simplistic solution on a deeper problem? Didn't the textbooks and renowned experts state that affection should be freely offered, not fought or shamed for?

Fingers trailed down her neck and she shivered free from her unsettling wondering.

This *was* different.

This was sexual desire.

And as Seve had already shown her, it had different rules. Different parameters.

For starters, this was fleeting. Between consenting adults.

And one night only.

Perhaps it was that simple. A giving and taking of carnal pleasure.

His searing gaze compelled her, his body poised in arrogant expectation.

'Please,' she tested, then felt a loud rush in her ears as his eyes lit up, his fingers stroking the leaping pulse at her throat. 'I want you. Please,' she whispered again.

A guttural groan of satisfaction was her reward. A feral sound she wouldn't have attributed to deepening her pleasure before tonight.

'It's my turn to demand more. Tell me what you want me to do to you, *bonita*.'

'Why?' she demanded again.

And that innocent query, that thirst for knowledge, made him harder than he'd ever been before.

His voice was barely coherent as he responded. 'Because it heightens *my* experience. Call it a primal thing if you want. But I need it.'

Wide eyes stared at him for a handful of seconds before they dropped to his mouth.

Seve could barely control his groan when she slicked her tongue over her lips and said, 'Please, kiss me again, Seve. I'm begging. I need more of everything you have to give.'

He was certain he slipped into temporary madness in that moment. Time, space and thought fled his consciousness.

He only *felt*. Experienced a depth of sensation he'd never considered possible.

With hands that shook from pure need, he peeled the dress off her body.

And was rewarded with a vision that siphoned every ounce of air from his lungs. *'Dulce cielo, eres hermosa,'* he praised, in a voice he didn't recognise.

His knees nearly buckled as he saw the surge of colour beneath her skin. As he gave in to the wild need and traced the flow with eager fingers. Revelled in her gasp as she begged some more.

With each lust-stoking plea, he kissed and licked and sucked, attempting gentleness that quickly fell by the wayside, propelled by primal hunger that demanded he leave his mark on this moment. On this woman.

She cried out when he suckled her pert, rose-tipped breasts, the Snow White replication of cream and rose driving him higher up the peak of insanity.

And when he'd kissed his way down her body and finally parted her thighs, the slick pink heart of her drove a pure, animal sound from his body. 'Every inch of you intoxicates me,' he confessed.

Her fingers curled into the rich coverlet, her back arching to his words. 'Show me, then. Please show me, Seve.' The tiny slur of her words, the rich Cardosian intonation of his name nearly undid him.

Like a starving man presented with a feast, he dropped onto his elbows, his arms shackling her supple thighs as he lowered his head. And feasted.

For as long as he lived, Seve suspected he would never forget the taste and feel of her, his plain-speaking genius with the untapped sensuality. A sensuality that unravelled into his waiting clutches, her husky cries a symphony he would remember long after this night.

Eager for more, more, more, he drove her from one peak to the other, her feminine core his priceless treasure.

'Please, I can't,' she protested weakly when he tried to command another release.

Drunk on her, he forced his head up, already missing the taste of her. 'Yes, you can. You will. I insist.'

The aftershocks simmering through her were a vision in and of themselves. He watched her hair ripple like a seductive river as her head thrashed on his pillow.

Allowing her the briefest respite, he rose and padded to his bedside table. The sensation of her eyes on him powered his unsated hunger as he tore open the condom and sheathed himself.

'You like what you see, *pequeña*?'

Her gaze dropped to his manhood and stared with unabashed wonder. 'Logic tells me you'll fit but I'm still a little…awed.'

Prowling back onto the bed, he arranged his logic-driven beauty so her sweet backside was tucked against him, one leg splayed over his and wide open to him. Wrapping one arm around her, he caught her arm and tucked it over his shoulder. With unfettered access to her front, Seve caught her earlobe in his teeth, his shaft throbbing when she shivered.

'Screw logic, *mi precioso*. Feel. Just *feel*.'

With that he hooked his arm beneath her knee and surged inside her. Her scream was a blessing and a curse. Because he wanted to hear more of it while lamenting that, like everything else about this captivating woman, it would remain imprinted on his psyche for the rest of his days.

Feel. Just *feel*.

Genie did nothing else for the next three hours. One moment blended into the other until she feared the fever possessing her would never break. That she would remain submerged in this alternative universe until she stopped breathing.

She discovered that the key code to unlocking Seve Valente's passion was to plead for pleasure. And she tapped it shamelessly.

A part of her suspected she revelled in this success because she'd failed in her primary goal, and his refusal still smarted. But the majority of it was because sex with Seve was unlike anything she'd experienced before.

Just as she knew it was something she wouldn't... *couldn't* repeat after this unique night was over. Like a rare comet streaking through the sky, this was as close to a once-in-a-lifetime event as she was likely to experience.

She'd witnessed first-hand through her parents how

impossible it was to satiate thirst-based pleasures. She'd
watched from the sidelines as they'd sought high after
high, each act more desperate than the last, the child
they used to fuel their proclivities forgotten.

It was why she'd vowed never to fall prey to such
addiction.

This…chemical reaction to Seve was one she would
wean herself from.

Now.

She forced her eyes open, stifling a moan when the
delicious heaviness in her limbs threatened to send her
into stupor once more.

He was sound asleep, his hair falling over his eyes.

Objectively she assessed him, willing her brain to
figure out why she'd reacted to him in such a *primal*
way. It wasn't because he'd provided for her in the archaic sense. Her attraction to him had started long before he'd astonished her by offering her over and above
her asking price. And as she'd said, this wasn't about
money.

Maybe this was one of those inexplicable enigmas.
Like why she loved the scent of patchouli but detested
the smell of lavender.

But, contrary to what he'd said before, she didn't
like puzzles. And he was a giant puzzle she needed to
set aside.

She had more important things to do.

So why was she lingering, fighting the urge to rake
back the lock of hair draping over his eyes? Why was
her gaze consuming every inch of tanned skin she could
see, reliving the feel of him beneath her touch?

Enough.

Their business was finished. Once she turned over

the sale to her lawyers she was done dealing with
Seve Valente.

For ten months at least.

A lot could happen in that time. If things went according to plan, she would have everything she'd
dreamed of.

A pang in her chest made her blink, and still she
couldn't drag her gaze from him.

If only he'd said yes…

The futile thought finally propelled her limbs into
motion. She told herself she didn't care whether he woke
or not but the very idea that she'd have to search for the
appropriate social cue, which she was entirely unaware
of, prompted her into stealth mode as she dressed and
went to fetch her clutch.

The code he'd imputed in the underground garage lift
was easy to recall and she used it to return to the lobby.
A few minutes after that, a taxi was ferrying her away
from the most stimulating night of her life.

Towards a future whose lights should've shone bright
but was inexplicably dimmed around the edges.

Nine weeks later

'The car is here to take you to the airport, Miss Merchant.'

Genie nodded, then tagged on her thanks, but she
didn't stop her progress through the sub-basement room
that had been her home for almost a decade.

For whatever small time remained, she let her gaze
wander over the almost empty space. She'd had her
computers placed in secure specialised storage until
she was eventually settled. But the memories were still

vivid. Some were agonising—like the weeks she'd been sure her very freedom was at stake—while others were exhilarating—like when she'd completed the first life-changing algorithm and test-driven it.

The remaining years had been sheer hard work, but it was work she'd relished with every fibre of her being because she'd believed every string of code would serve a greater good.

And she'd done it.

She had achieved one long-desired goal. She'd ticked items off her years-old to-do list.

The contract with Valente Ventures was done and dusted.

Silicon Valley and the world media had lauded her achievement with superlatives. She'd been welcome into the Ten-Digit Club with more offers than she could count. Several megalomaniacs had immediately attempted to hire her, just so they could harness her power.

She'd ignored them all.

Only to be stuck at the final hurdle. She'd allowed her assistant to keep the flight booking only because she hadn't been able to wrestle her whirling thoughts long enough to formulate a new plan.

Her current situation had fully stymied her and forced her into suspended animation. She couldn't make firm plans until she knew. And with each day she delayed finding out, the deeper she sank into inertia.

To say she was disappointed in herself was an understatement. Especially since within that understatement existed an electric current of trepidation, humming and buzzing its presence that wouldn't leave her alone. Because if she did confirm what she suspected was happening, she'd have no choice but to act on the data. Specifically—

'Miss Merchant, sorry to disturb you but there's someone here to see you.'

She didn't need to turn around to *know*. It was almost laughable that it should happen like this. Just like last time.

Except this time, she was deep in her natural habitat. A place she deemed sacred. Her sanctuary. If only for a short while longer.

But Seve Valente's air of entitlement was total. He strode into her tech lab as if he owned it. Because he did.

She watched him walk around, broad-shouldered and viscerally masculine, those piercing eyes stripping every corner, every socket and cubbyhole as if he had the rights to its secrets. To *her* secrets.

Part of her was thankful he'd never ventured down here when she was surrounded by her treasured possessions, devices that had saved her from a life of apathy and abject hopelessness.

He would've seen too much then. *Still* saw too much now.

Probably labelled her pathetic hermit, more attached to gadgets than to human beings, the way her father once scathingly did. All because she wouldn't embrace financial success the way he thought she should.

Reminding herself that those times were behind her, that this connection with Seve Valente would also soon be behind her, she forced composure into her body and turned, attempted to stare him down.

Despite the complete lack of readiness for the atomic impact of him.

Despite wanting nothing more than the freedom to re-live every single moment of their time in his penthouse.

A freedom she couldn't afford.

'You have no right to be here.' She didn't add *not yet* because it was elementary. She'd signed the papers two weeks ago. His fourteen-day grace period ended at midday.

It was now eleven fifty-four.

But she suspected the remaining six minutes weren't what was uppermost in his mind when his gaze scoured her from head to toe before returning to her face.

'Oh, I have every right. As part of our contract, I now own this building. Which gives me the right to be inside it.'

Heat flooded her body. Was he playing with her by using those words?

'But you don't own everyone *in* it. You don't own me. You could've waited a few more minutes and I would've been gone. Why didn't you?'

Something raw and primal shimmered over his face, sending shivers through her body. 'I'm here because as much as I want to ignore the possibility of what may have occurred, I've recognised that only direct communication will serve in learning the truth. So here I am.'

Her heart dipped, pretended to fail then righted itself again. 'I'm not a mind-reader, Mr Valente. You're going to have to spell out what you mean.'

The smallest fraction of a smile twitched one corner of his mouth. 'Of course. As you wish, *pequeña.*' He sauntered closer, bringing his scent with him, along with proof that, in some instances, chemistry could be replicated with the same astounding results.

Because she was breathing him in, relishing the uniquely pleasing scent.

'The last time we were together, we made love for hours in my bed. I have no reason to believe the contraception failed but the experience was more…intense than I expected. With resulting recklessness.'

Heat punched through her at his words, vivid reminders exploding across her brain like the fireworks she sometimes watched from her bedroom window on New Year's.

'We would've discussed it if you hadn't chosen to leave without the courtesy of saying goodbye.' He eyed her with something close to condemnation, a flicker of something almost…harrowing passing over his features before he continued. 'Now, I'd like to believe that nothing came of it and your silence since then suggests so. But some things I'd prefer not to leave to chance. So I'm here to ask you, Genie. Is there something I need to know? Are you leaving with something that belongs to me?'

'Everything that is exclusively yours is already signed over to you,' she returned heatedly, well aware she was evading the question.

Seve Valente was equally astute, perhaps even more than her genius IQ since he had the backing of worldly experience she readily admitted she sorely lacked. So she wasn't surprised when his eyes narrowed. 'I assure you, this isn't the time to play semantics with me. If you have something I have rights to, Genie, now's the time to confess it. Do you?'

Seve watched nerves take hold of her for a few seconds, but as expected, and as had so intrigued him about this breathtaking creature, she didn't back down. If anything, she stepped up, her chin angling up so she could flay him with her gaze. It was fiercely enraging—and furiously unacceptable—that the move aroused him to the point of breath-stealing intensity.

'I have nothing to confess, since I don't know myself.'

His eyes narrowed. 'You don't know? It's been nine weeks. Which makes your ignorance deliberate. Because you're hoping that by staying in the dark, *I'll* go away?'

Her heating cheeks betrayed her.

He laughed, a low, hoarse sound that made her eyes widen. 'You're not that deluded, Genie, surely?'

She bit her lip and the wildness straining through his veins threatened to explode. For weeks he'd dismissed this sensation every time she crossed his mind, steeped in his unshakeable belief that it was only a matter of time before it dissipated. But here he was, confronted by the unwavering truth.

He still wanted Genie Merchant. Desperately. Ferociously.

Once hadn't been nearly enough.

Hell, not even the prohibitive thought that she might be carrying his child, a notion he'd never wanted but could now not go more than five minutes without obsessing over, could kill his rampant lust for her.

'I have a plane to catch, Mr Valente.'

Her glib dismissal turned his mood darker, the hollow in his gut at the thought that she might *not* be pregnant bewildering him now as when she'd issued that absurd condition weeks ago. But she still *hadn't* denied it. 'You'll do well to cooperate with me, Genie.'

'My social cues may be lacking but that sounds like a threat.'

He smiled. 'It's an offer of advice I suggest you take.'

'I told you I don't have any news for you, and I meant it. When I learn otherwise, I'll let you know. That's the best I can offer. Besides, you weren't interested in aiding me in having a baby. I'm assuming this is just a cursory interest that will wane with time.'

'You assume wrong. Refusing to participate in creating a child is one thing. Creating one anyway regardless of circumstances is another.' And if they had...if his child was, even at this moment, growing in her belly...

Cold sweat prickled the back of his neck as disturbing memories threatened to crowd in again. Was he resilient enough to stop past trauma from staining a new, innocent life?

The question was still quaking through him when she nodded briskly.

'Understood. Goodbye, Mr Valente.'

For far longer than was polite, he stared at her. Genie didn't need a string of source code to decipher that she wouldn't like whatever was brewing in his formidable mind.

But since she didn't intend to be around for it...

Clutching her bag to her body, she headed for the door, making sure to stay out of arm's reach of the man who continued to dominate far too much of her thoughts. With every step, she felt his gaze boring deeper into her.

She didn't breathe until she was safely ensconced in the lift. Even then she remained wary, her gaze darting around her when she reached the lobby. All the way to her ear, she expected large hands to grab her, shackle her to his hard, warm body.

But she wasn't stopped.

Forty minutes later, when a smiling stewardess approached her in the first-class lounge to inform her that her plane was boarding, she breathed a sigh of relief.

And mild disappointment.

For all his bluster and stern pronouncements, Seve Valente had let her slip free despite suspecting she might be carrying his child.

For weeks, he'd lived with the possibility that she might be pregnant and done nothing about it. He might have felt obliged to bring it up but he'd effortlessly let himself off the hook at her smallest resistance.

In the end, his new acquisition was all he'd been interested in.

Just as the financial rewards of her genius had been all her parents craved.

Logic stated that she should be relieved with this outcome.

Except *logical* was far from what she felt as she followed the attendant down a surprisingly deserted ramp.

With illogical and emotional thoughts crowding her mind, she barely noticed that the plane was far smaller than the one she'd expected.

That the interior was plush to the point of luxury. That it, like the ramp, was devoid of passengers. But most importantly, that the attendant was shutting the door and the engine was already powering up.

By the time logic rushed in and lit up neon signs in her brain, the attendant was disappearing into a galley.

A door was opening at the back of the plane.

The figure walking towards her none other than Seve

Valente, fire and brimstone and ruthless determination stamped into every inch of his body.

Her gaze whipped around her before returning to his. 'Wh-what are you...? What in heaven's name is going on?'

He stopped two feet from her. Slate-grey eyes consumed her from head to toe, as if he hadn't seen her less than an hour ago. After an eternity, he reached out and relieved her of her bag, tossing it aside. Then he wrapped his hands around her arms and urged her shock-riddled body into the nearest club seat.

With quick, efficient motion, he secured the seat belt.

Only then did he lean close and murmur in her ear, 'I told you I always get what I want. You should've believed me.'

'No.'

The single word injected her with adrenaline that punched the shock right out of her. Unfortunately, it was too late. The plane, which she now registered was a very sleek, private jet, was already in motion.

'*Sí, pequeña.* We've been given permission to take off. There is no going back.'

'Stop calling me that. I'm not your sweetheart.'

His jaw clenched, his eyes gleaming in a way that said her self-preservation instincts needed to be at peak performance. She'd illogically assumed her sharp exit had concluded their business and lowered her guard.

The reminder of her flawed thinking made her hand scramble for her seat belt, belatedly spurred into action.

With lightning-quick reflexes, he surged forward and placed his hands over hers. 'Stop. We're about to take off. You will remain seated.' His tone was unbending steel.

'Subterfuge, then throwing commands at me. I guess now you have my algorithm there's no need to hide your true colours, is there?'

One eyebrow cocked. 'How have I deceived you?'

She waved a wild hand at the window and the view trundling past at speed. 'Are you serious? You're in the middle of kidnapping me! Stop the plane right now!'

His smile was lethal. And pulse-shredding. 'I will not. I gave you ample warning,' he murmured almost softly, as if he pitied her for not heeding him.

'And this is the solution you came up with? To detain me against my will?'

'Until I find out whether you're carrying my child or not? Yes.' His eyes narrowed. 'Tell me why you haven't taken a pregnancy test yet.'

She swallowed. 'I don't owe you an explanation.'

His lips thinned. 'Then prepare to not be let out of my sight until we know one way or the other.'

'What?'

'Your hearing is perfectly fine, Genie.'

She looked out of the window at the swiftly disappearing landscape as if it would give her insight as to how deep his madness went. 'Where are you taking me?'

'That depends on a few outcomes.'

She laughed but the sound abruptly cut off when his gaze dropped to the hand she'd placed unwittingly on her flat belly. 'You mean you'll drop me off in Paris and you can go on your merry way to wherever once we verify I'm not pregnant?'

His gaze shot up to her. 'You think you're not?'

The laser-sharp intensity to the question made her breath catch because it held notes she couldn't quite decipher. Notes that sounded like disappointment…*but not quite*. Like the merest hint of loss…mourning…*but not quite*. 'I told you, I don't know.'

As was becoming customary in their interaction, he let the silence stretch out for uncomfortable seconds while his gaze roamed over her face. Her hair. The tightly woven fingers in her lap. Then back up to her mouth.

Genie wanted to scream at him that she wasn't a museum oddity to be examined quite so thoroughly. But…she'd never experienced anything like it before they met nine weeks ago.

She still hadn't.

And social cues or not, the way this man—vastly worldly, visually arresting and far too arrogant with it, who knew he commanded female interest just by breathing—watched her was…addictive.

After minutes had passed, during which the aircraft soared into the skies, setting her heart racing faster, he looked over her shoulder.

Following his gaze, she saw the attendant who'd walked her onto the plane emerge from the galley. The attendant nodded at Seve and smiled at her.

'Can I get you anything, Miss Merchant?'

The tart, intensely antisocial response rose and died on her tongue. She couldn't take out her angry panic on an attendant doing her job.

About to shake her head, she glared at Seve when he murmured, 'Some water would be great, Agnetha. Thanks.'

With another courteous smile, the attendant hurried to do her master's bidding.

'I commend you for holding your tongue,' he drawled.

She glared harder. 'I don't make a habit of attacking people who don't deserve it.'

His teeth bared in a breathtaking caricature of a smile. 'That's good to hear. We may have room for peaceful negotiation yet.'

'Any negotiation between us was forfeit when you kidnapped me, Mr Valente.'

'Seve,' he insisted with a glint in his eyes that sent shivers over her body.

'We're not friends. I won't pretend otherwise.'

Another slow scrutiny of her face and body. 'But we've been much more, *pequeña*.'

'A mistake you'll recall I was eager to put behind me by leaving before morning.'

His face hardened, but his words were still silky smooth when he responded, 'Are you sure that's why you left?'

She snorted. 'Why else?'

'Because you found our night as stimulating as I did, perhaps? I was there, remember. You were insatiable, *bonita*. Breathtakingly so.' One hand rose from where it'd been resting on his hard-packed belly to his lips, his fingers tracing over his lower lip.

As if reliving their kiss.

Heat swelled and pulsed between her thighs as she watched, unwillingly mesmerised as his finger moved back and forth over his velvet-smooth lower lip.

Whatever pithy answer she'd tried to conjure up withered under the force of sensation pummelling her and, in its place, a traitorous moan started to rise. Genie swallowed quickly, dragging her gaze away to notice that they'd levelled off.

She was further saved from answering when the attendant returned with a crystal-cut glass and a carafe of water.

Just for something to do, Genie took the drink, murmuring her thanks before raising to sip, keenly aware of Seve watching her every move.

She drained the glass, then, that vexing compulsion striking again, she glanced at him. To find him watching her with unabashed satisfaction.

'What?' she barked, the sensation that she'd done exactly as he'd wanted swirling through her.

He didn't respond immediately. His gaze went to the window, then the moment a muted ping sounded in the cabin, he rose and held out his hand.

'Come with me.'

She remained seated. 'Not a chance in hell, Mr Valente.'

He dropped his hand, and she breathed a sigh of relief. Only to have it snatched away when he stepped close and dropped into a smooth squat before her.

Standing tall, he'd been formidable, a pillar of masculinity that drew unfair attention to him.

Crouched before her, in a diminishing position that didn't diminish this man even one iota, he made her want to do the unthinkable. To reach out and cup that marble-hard jaw. To experience the heat and power of him. Chafe her skin against the delicious stubble springing to life over his vibrant olive skin.

Before their meeting nine weeks ago, she'd had minimal human contact. Went out of her way to avoid it unless strictly necessary.

Seve Valente had delivered a feast on which she had gorged until her every sense was saturated. After which she had gone back to hungering.

Now, like an addict, she was desperate to feel again. He'd opened her eyes and her senses to a world she couldn't sever herself from. With each moment in his presence, it grew impossible.

His words slammed into her memory.

Screw logic. Feel. Just feel.

'Let's not prolong this any longer, Genie,' he said with heavy finality.

Cold reality rushed in. While she'd been lost in their torrid night together, he'd leaned in closer, his gaze devouring her once more. His hands were positioned on either side of her hips without touching, and, that absurdly, it made her yearn for contact all that much more.

He's *kidnapping* you.

The forceful reminder brought welcome clarity of thought. As much as she wanted to refuse, she knew he was formidable. Seve wasn't about to let this go until he had her cooperation.

She could protest all she wanted, but the only way she'd rid herself of him was to bend a little while she was forced on this flight with him.

Once they landed however…

'Fine,' she said, thankful when her voice emerged even, betraying nothing of what she'd been feeling for the last few minutes.

Just as quickly, he disengaged her seat belt and rose. This time he didn't hold out his hand to her, the absence of which she felt distinctly as she stood and followed him at a slower place to the back of the plane.

When she realised he was entering a sleeping cabin, she froze in the doorway.

Did he think…? Surely he wasn't that deluded?

She opened her mouth to ask the very same question, ignoring the flash of heat and anticipation zipping through her body as he came towards her.

'These weren't the circumstances under which I imagined we would conclude this conversation, but here we are,' he drawled.

She felt the blood drain from her head when she saw the packages in his hand. 'You're not serious.'

CHAPTER FOUR

HE MERELY RAISED an eyebrow, delivering a pithy answer with that smooth motion.

'You want me to take a pregnancy test right now? Absolutely not!' Raised voice. Elevated heartbeat. Vivid sensation pulsing through her. All signs of unstructured overstimulation.

Absently, Genie wondered why she wasn't more alarmed. Why she felt weirdly...*alive*.

Granted, she'd also never been pregnant—a possibility she suspected was most likely. Nevertheless, she blamed him entirely for her destabilised state because, according to the information she'd consumed, pregnancy hormones wouldn't kick in for another week or two.

'This plane's travelling range is thirteen and a half hours. I'm sure you'd like to finish this business long before then.'

She balled her fist. 'I have a right to do this in my own time.'

'Then why haven't you done it yet?' He raised a hand when she opened her mouth to shut him down. 'Before you say it, this no longer falls under the "none of your business" banner.'

She bit her tongue. As much as she wanted to hate him, he was right. Hell, she had the same superior brand of test he held in his hand burning a hole in her handbag.

'Tell me why,' he urged.

She hated him even more because he didn't demand or command. There was genuine curiosity in his tone. A need to know that urged her to confront her own reasons why.

She was afraid.

Afraid that, despite wanting this more than she'd ever wanted anything else, she would fall short as a mother. That the same lack her parents had found in her would curtail her full potential as a parent.

She was different. She knew that in her bones. An oddity in a world that rarely celebrated idiosyncrasies unless they directly benefitted or entertained, and even then, preferring the benefits to be delivered from a distance. As much as she hated to admit it, that difference had chipped away at her self-esteem over the years.

Enough to make her put this off even after two missed periods.

She couldn't tell Seve any of this, of course. The raw power he exuded and the conquer-at-all-costs persona demanded that she keep her fears under lock and key.

So she cast her gaze around the room. Then forced a shrug. 'I wasn't ready.'

His eyes narrowed and his body turned stiff as marble. 'You weren't ready?' he repeated with zero emotion. 'You asked me to father your child as part of our deal nine weeks ago.'

The memory burned and chafed inside her, the bold attraction that had led her to issue that request still disarming. 'I did. And had you said yes, we would've discussed the appropriate time for scheduling a baby.'

Impossibly, he grew stiffer and, from the corner of her eye, she watched his face turn dark with condemnation. '*Scheduling a baby?* Like scheduling a coffee run or a test drive on a string of code?' he bit out, his tone arctic.

Like last time, she'd evidently struck a nerve. Again, she tried to see beneath his surface to why he felt so strongly about it.

Since he'd said no.

'Well, not as unfeeling as all that but—'

'But what? You would've found time to schedule in some emotion too?'

Despite deliberately seeking the distance from emotion, Genie felt her insides sting at his words. 'How I feel about the child I may or may not be carrying is—'

'Let me guess, none of my business? That's where you're wrong. Because now more than ever, I'm convinced right here is where I need to be,' he stated with rigid reproach. 'Let me state again. I'm not going anywhere, Genie. Not until we confirm whether or not you're carrying my child. So what's it to be?'

Get it over and done with.

She wanted to deny the voice echoing in her head.

But she'd strung this out long enough. Her life was going to change whether she liked it or not. Hell, she'd already adopted her eating, sleeping and exercising habits to accommodate the possible pregnancy. If she was preparing her body for the biggest event of her life, then she couldn't bury her head in the sand any longer.

Her heart hammered with mild panic as he held out the packages to her.

In less than five minutes she would know whether she was going to be a mother.

They both would.

Her hand shook as she took them from him. She barely saw him motion towards the door that led to the plane's bathroom. But she was searingly aware of him following a few steps behind her until he stopped himself, his hands forcibly shoved into the pockets of his trousers.

Genie didn't need to look over her shoulder to know that his gaze was boring into her, its intensity very much heightened.

Contrary to what she'd thought, he was heavily invested, she realised. Or else he wouldn't have taken such drastic actions.

Shutting the door behind her, she shook her head. It didn't matter. Her plans about her child had never included its father. She was sure she could negotiate Seve out of this too, if it came to it.

Is that wise?

She bunched a fist over the sink, avoiding her own gaze as she shook her head once again. It didn't matter. Single parenthood had been the plan all along. Once she got over this alarm, the merits would be just the same.

Running her gaze over the instructions twice, she tore the box open and took the test. After washing her hands, she sat on the lid of the toilet, every cell in her body shaking as the endless seconds ticked by.

Five minutes later, she stared at the thick cross that positively confirmed what she already knew deep in her heart.

Uneven waves of panic, awe and disbelief washed over her until she wasn't sure which emotions she was drowning under. Raising her eyes to the mirror, she caught sight of her glazed eyes, her pale face, the breaths puffing out of her stunned mouth.

She was pregnant.

'Genie.'

The naked blade of his voice, edged with simmering emotions she couldn't name, cut through the euphoric fog of her brain.

She was pregnant.

She fumbled for the door. She expected him to rush in, but he remained aloof a few steps away. An omen, perhaps?

Maybe not, if the fever blazing in his eyes was any indication. He didn't even need to voice the question. It was a towering neon sign growing larger by the second.

'Yes. I'm pregnant.' The words fell like tiny, explosive miracles from her lips.

A loud rush followed, drowning out all sound. The plane pitched. Or maybe it was her.

Genie wasn't entirely sure as she took a step and fell forward into pitch darkness.

When she blinked awake, she was in the king-size bed, fat pillows propped behind her, and thick luxurious covers thrown over her body.

Seve sat on the edge, tension vibrating from his body as he stared down at the test confirming the altered course of her life.

Of *their* lives.

No. She had enough to contend with. She wasn't going to allow her brain to accommodate what this meant for Seve too.

She raised a hand to her temple, struggling to sit up. 'Wh-what happened?'

Sizzling eyes shifted from the stick to her face, conducting a quick scrutiny. 'You announced you were pregnant, then passed out,' he gritted out.

Pregnant...

The power of that word was...indescribable.

Her hand trailed to her stomach. He followed the movement, his face clenching as he exhaled.

'Dear God, I did *not* just swoon like a pathetic Victorian maiden,' she muttered.

He heard her, of course. He was attuned to her in a way that should've been uncanny, and yet, the more exposed she was to it, the more she accepted it.

'Let's blame it on turbulence,' he rasped. His face remained grave but she had the absurd urge to laugh. A broken sound escaped before she could stop it.

His eyes latched onto her throat, as if he yearned to hear it again.

Shaking her head, she reached for the covers, ready to throw them off.

'Stay.'

It wasn't an arrogant command like before; nevertheless it was a directive that made her bristle. She needed solitude to properly absorb the news. To talk herself through this trepidation so she could make careful plans for her baby. 'Haven't we achieved the objective of all of this?'

He rested his elbows on his knees, subtly blocking her exit from this side of the bed. 'We've merely verified the foundation on which we stand.'

'What does that mean?'

He didn't answer. Instead, he reached for a sleek little gadget on the bedside table. She watched him press the button labelled 'cockpit' with growing alarm.

The crisp voice answered, echoing in the room. 'Yes, sir?'

'Flight option one, please,' Seve responded.

'Of course, Mr Valente.'

He released the button, then eyed her in a way that made the hairs on her nape stand up.

'Flight option one?' Even as she repeated it, Genie suspected she wouldn't like what it meant. 'For your sake I hope that means you're delivering me to my original destination.'

One corner of his mouth lifted but there was no humour in the motion. 'I'm sorry to disappoint you, but no. We flew over Norway about half an hour ago.'

'Then turn back!'

The tic in his jaw gave her his answer even before he said, 'No. You're carrying my child. That changes things.'

'What things—?' The question snagged in her throat as the aircraft banked with a definite course adjustment that made her heart lurch. 'Why is your pilot changing course? Where are we going?'

He rose from the bed, and she noticed the pregnancy test was still in his hand. He stared down at it for a long moment, his chest rising and falling in heavy breathing. Then he speared her with ferocious eyes, his stance giving no quarter as he answered. 'We're going to Cardosia. Where my child will be born.'

Several thoughts charged through her brain as she stared at him.

The primary one was that *this* was why she didn't like human interaction. Because half of the time she wasn't sure whether they were the faulty creatures, or *she* was missing vital clues of fairness and decency.

'You're quite insane if you think I'm going anywhere with you, never mind staying for the better part of a year.'

Her scathing response didn't faze him one iota. 'As far as I know, insanity doesn't run in my family. Which is why I can assure you with one hundred per cent certainty that that's exactly what is going to happen.'

She swallowed the unhelpful panic scrabbling at her throat. 'Enlighten me, please. Is this usual behaviour for men like you?'

'I don't speak for other men, nor do I care how the general male population feel about anything. You're my main concern. And you, Genie Merchant, are in the unique position of being the only woman who has affected me enough for me to lose my head in bed. Just as you are the unique woman carrying my child.'

Her nails dug into the covers, seeking an anchor in this mad tempest. '*Our* child. If you must make proprietary assertions, have the decency to include me.'

'Perhaps I do so because I suspect that if you had your way, you would put the distance of half a world between me and what's mine.'

She couldn't deny it. Nor could she stop the treacherous heat that confirmed his words. 'Well, calling it your child doesn't make it so.'

He gave a slow, eloquent shrug that emphasised every step he was taking to stake his claim. And in that shrug, she learned something else.

Seve Valente wasn't about to budge an iota.

He surged forward when she threw her legs over the side of the bed and stood up, but he didn't touch her. He watched her like a hawk however. And she realised he'd stayed close long enough to ensure she wouldn't topple over again.

It shouldn't have chipped at a small fraction of her fury. That it did bewildered her even more. This man was making declarations about her life while keeping her prisoner on his airborne palace. Every cell in her body should be incandescent.

Yet several of those cells strained towards him as she passed him. Even more infuriating, a significant portion of her senses delighted in his scent, the aura emanating from him, as she noted that the delicious stubble had grown even more. Wondered how deliciously it would chafe if she—

No!

She was absolutely not going down that unhinged path. It was what had landed her here after all.

One night. It was only meant to be one night.

She realised she'd said it out loud when his whole body tightened, turning even more marble-like than before.

'But a night with consequences, evidently.'

'Why are you doing this? You don't even want a child. You said as much.'

His eyes glinted, his incisive gaze tracking her as she paced the small cabin. 'What I felt a few weeks ago no longer matters.'

'That's absurd. Of course it does.'

He gritted his teeth. 'Let me rephrase. The child you're carrying…my child, is now my number one priority. I'm not taking eyes off you until he or she is born.'

Something inside her cracked against her will, and without her permissions started to melt. Since she couldn't fathom what it was, she immediately took steps to shore it up. To separate it from clear, logical thinking. She couldn't afford anything else.

Couldn't afford to wonder how her life's trajectory would've changed if only her parents had made her their number one priority.

They hadn't. They'd put her last on their list every time.

Until she'd taken herself off it completely. Until she'd emotionally emancipated herself from the two people who should've given her unconditional love and support but had only zealously loved her bank balance.

They'd helped themselves to her millions, citing that they'd given their lives and livelihood for her dream and therefore were entitled to it.

'And what happens after that? Your end goal currently seems to be delivery.'

'That will be a matter for later discussion.' Although he didn't break their stare, Genie got the singular feeling he'd already made up his mind. That he was several steps ahead of her and was keeping that vital move to himself. 'For now all you need to know is that you're going to be in a place where you're provided with a healthy diet and strict monitoring that doesn't include living in an underground tech dungeon where you ignore the existence of sunlight and human interaction for weeks on end.'

The wave of desolation and hurt that swept through her took her literal breath away. She managed to snatch it back, as she whirled around and headed for the door.

'Where are you going? We're not done talking, Genie.'

She grasped the door handle and rapidly blinked away stupid tears. 'Logic tells me that if I find your words hurtful and disrespectful then we shouldn't engage in conversation.'

'Or, contrarily, we should keep talking until there's no room for doubt.'

His deep voice right over her shoulder indicated he'd followed her. And really? There was nowhere to go. Her only option was to have this conversation within earshot of the attendants.

When Genie turned he was, as expected, only three feet away. She grasped at the last tendrils of composure and went to the nearest seat set next to the window. 'I don't owe you explanation on how I live my life but, if you must know, I exercise three times a week and have been exceptionally prudent with my diet the last few weeks.'

Perhaps she was mistaken but his shoulders relaxed a tiniest fraction at her words. '*Bueno*. But you fainted a little while ago. This baby is already making demands on your body, so I need to know how you feel. And not just physically. Emotionally too.'

'I could tell you that. I could also shout and ask where you get the nerve to ask me that. But why would I hand you the advantage of any of that? You said unapologetically that you're not above using my feelings to manipulate me into giving you what you want.'

He didn't respond, merely crossed his arms over his sculpted chest, leaned back against the door and watched her.

Genie considered sitting in silence right along with him. But Dr Douglas's voice chose that moment to gently chide her.

Take the high road.

Casting a glance out of the window so he wouldn't

see how much the words affected her, she kept her gaze on the fluffy clouds as she answered. 'Okay. I feel lonely. A lot. All the time, actually. Even when my parents were alive.'

A furtive glance out of the corner of her eye showed his arms had dropped, a disarmed look on his face.

She'd shocked Seve Valente with her unguarded honesty.

It wasn't a terrible feeling. So she went further. 'I felt lonely even before I was old enough to understand what that feeling meant. It hasn't gone away.'

Seve prowled closer, emotion in his eyes she couldn't quite decipher. 'That's why you wanted a child?' he grated out.

'Partly.'

'What other reasons are there?' he pressed, not giving any quarter now she'd cracked the door open.

'Because I'm aware of where my parents went wrong, and I'm well equipped to not repeat their mistakes.'

'Doing the opposite of what they did wouldn't automatically guarantee the results you require,' he countered, a bite in his voice.

She turned from the window to face him. 'I wasn't planning on using the exact opposite template. Just doing things differently.'

His nostrils flared in irritation. 'You could still go wrong elsewhere, unless you have the answer to every question being a parent entails. And that's impossible.'

'I know being a good parent doesn't come from books. It comes from within.' She knew that deep in her soul because that was where the most anguishing hurt had resided. 'What about you? You're so busy labelling me an unfit parent five minutes after discovering you're going to be a father. What experience do you have to show that you'll do any better?'

His jaw tightened when the accusation hit the mark. Shadows of bleakness and bitterness charted over his face, but he tossed them off almost instantly. 'Unlike you, I'm willing to admit I don't have all the answers—'

'And yet you're determined to emerge the winner.'

His nostrils flared in displeasure. 'For starters, I have a better support system. And this isn't about winning—'

'Of course it is. You see the child I'm carrying as yours. You're taking it away because you believe you're better equipped to take care of it than I am.'

'As opposed to what? Having it brought up on some grey corner of your AI lab where you can nip in and check on it in between building algorithms?'

The sting in her midriff intensified. 'Your views are based on nothing but assumptions.'

'Prove me wrong, then. Show me how wrong I am.'

'You're baiting me into showing my hand again.'

He shrugged. 'You have to reveal your cards at some point, Genie. You can't hold them to your chest and expect me to take you at your word. What were your plans to bring up my…our baby?'

'What are yours? Beside kidnapping and holding me hostage for the duration of my pregnancy?'

Purpose rippled from him in waves. And somehow, she wasn't at all surprised when he merely rasped, 'You'll find out soon enough.'

He was doing the right thing.

Whenever the tiny pinpricks of guilt lanced him, he pushed back. *Hard.* Because he couldn't afford even an ounce of softening. Not when the stakes were this high.

He glanced at the closed cabin door and tightened his resolve.

Genie had coldly frozen him out once it became clear he wasn't changing his mind about their destination or revealing his plans for the baby she carried.

For his child.

He clenched his gut against the next shockwave that surged at those three words. But even more shocking? The fact that, watching her walking into the bathroom to perform the test, he'd felt a punch of dismay at the possibility of the result being negative.

Nine weeks ago he'd dismissed her request for a child as insane because the notion of fathering a child had been anathema to him. A deliberately abstract occurrence he'd been certain he wouldn't mind if it never came to pass.

Waking up the morning after their night together to find her gone, he'd convinced himself that it was for the best, too. Hell, he'd been saved the firm but awkward disentangling from clinging expectations.

That flash of disgruntlement that had lingered far longer than he'd wanted it to? It'd weirdly been allayed when, replaying their night together in the shower, he'd been jolted by the possibility that the protection had failed beneath the vigour of their coming together. He'd remained in that shower far longer than usual, alternately shocked and alarmed by the thought that he was in no hurry to chase after Genie Merchant to verify.

Even the primal urge to ensure she made the choice he preferred had disappeared at the certainty that if she was pregnant, she would keep the child.

His child.

He'd been in no hurry because *that* had meant he'd

see her again, one way or another. If only to verify that their night together had left no consequence.

It was that very unsettling notion that refused to dissipate, urging strongly that theirs was unfinished business, aside from the algorithm contract, that had conversely kept him away until the very last moment.

Had he known subconsciously that this life-changing event was on the horizon?

He shook his head. What did it matter now? The only material thing going forward was that he was going to be a father. With the crushing weight of history a jagged spear in his chest.

Would he fail his child just as his parents had done? Would he at some point in the future lose his way so badly that he wouldn't care whether his child was harmed by another so long as it benefitted *him*?

It might seem unthinkable to him *now* but what of the future when he didn't know how his twisted childhood would manifest itself?

His lungs constricted again with deep apprehension but he pulled himself past it.

It wouldn't happen. Not if he took the steps he was planning.

For a start, it was even more imperative now that the future stability of Cardosia was ensured. Disabling his uncle's hold on his homeland was one way of ensuring his flesh and blood had a future home and legacy. Something to be proud of if all else failed. One thing that wouldn't make Seve a failure in his child's eyes.

Glancing at the door one last time, he rose and went in the opposite direction, towards the plane's conference room. As much as he would like Genie's cooperation in all this, he was prepared for there to be a little turbulence before the path smoothed out.

He was used to adversity. And between the baby growing in the womb of the woman in his cabin and his determination to save Cardosia, he would have a battle on his hands.

Accepting that, he opened his laptop and brought up the latest weekly report on his uncle's activities.

The very first page darkened his mood.

Between last week and this, Lorenzo Valente had brokered two more deals that would strip essential resources from Cardosia's ecosystem. Even worse, Seve knew every cent of that deal would be funnelled into his uncle's private bank account in Luxembourg.

By the time he reached the end of the twenty-three-page document, fury blazed through his bloodstream.

Snatching up the phone, he punched in the far too well-used numbers. The moment it was answered, he barked, 'Have you seen the latest report?'

'We have, sir. We're attempting to stall the deals he's making but we won't be able to do so for ever. He's the head of state.'

His fingers tightened around the phone. '*Dios mio.* Try harder! This is unacceptable.'

He'd been used as a pawn as a child and, even as a successful man, Seve knew Lorenzo still flaunted his name about in order to secure deals for himself. His wily uncle continued to pillage his homeland ceaselessly.

No more.

The team he'd put together to monitor his uncle's activities—and to stall his intentions to bleed Cardosia dry—comprised scientists, economists and a few key figures serving in his uncle's government

The oldest of them was the one who bore the misnomer of a conscientious politician—Alfredo Santiago. He cleared his throat and Seve pinched the bridge of his nose because he knew what was coming. Alfredo never failed to bring it up at least once in their every interaction.

'You know what you need to do, son. The window of opportunity is fast closing.'

'And I've told you, I'm not going to run for president.'

'Can you afford not to? Soon there will be no Cardosia left to find on a map. Hell, he was heard floating the idea that our beloved country should become a province of one of her larger and more powerful neighbours.'

His chest clenched. 'What? Are you serious?'

'I'm an old man, Seve. I can't afford jokes when the stakes are this high.'

'And I'm telling you to focus your energies in that regard elsewhere. Cardosia will be in more capable hands than mine. Politics bore me to death.'

The old man snorted. 'Says the man who's livid at what's happening to his homeland. If that isn't what pure passion of a patriot looks like, then I've led a very wasted life thus far.'

Pure passion.

He hated that those two words threw up a different image. That of having Genie Merchant underneath him, of pumping into her tight sheath as she screamed her pleasure. Unadulterated pleasure expressed without an ounce of manufactured performance.

Seve shifted in his seat when his blood rushed south and awoke senses he didn't need awakened right this minute. Clearing his throat, he forced his focus on the conversation. On the utter abomination of what his uncle was doing to Cardosia. 'Tell me who Lorenzo has been speaking to. I need to know who to put on my red list.'

'A red list is all well and good, Seve. But you're attacking the symptom instead of the disease. I know you don't want to consider it, but you really are our only hope. Time is fast running out.'

His nape tingled with dread at the finality in the man's tone.

Long after that conversation had ended, Seve was reminded that one of the reasons he liked dealing with Santiago was because he didn't exaggerate or overdramatise a situation. Which meant things were as dire as stated. Perhaps even more so.

Gritting his teeth, he placed the next call on his list, making no bones about the consequences for those who supported his uncle in his efforts in hastening Cardosia towards perilous straits. His last was to the private bank he knew his uncle used. But even as he threatened fire and brimstone, he knew there was only so much his threats would achieve.

Which was why he was still locked in full frustration mode three hours later when he ordered lunch for Genie and, tray in hand, retraced his steps.

She was sitting up in bed when he entered, her hair a little tousled and the remnants of sleep in her eyes. Slivers of sunlight slanting through the windows formed a halo around her and his gut clenched against the enticing picture she made in his bed with his covers and pillows tossed around her.

It would have been no effort at all to set the tray to

one side, to prowl onto the bed, nudge her back against
the pillows and take his fill of that satin-soft mouth.
Would she gasp and moan as she had nine weeks ago?
Would those bottomless green eyes reflect every facet
of her pleasure as she clung to him?

Si. She would. He was sure of it. Her unfettered passion lurked just beneath her no-nonsense surface, waiting to be reignited to life.

Except if he attempted such a thing, she would probably claw his eyes out, considering the glare she was di-
recting his way. For now, he needed her less…stressed
about his intention to install her fully in his life. At least
until the baby arrived.

'You're awake. *Bueno.*'

Striding across the room, he frowned down at the
tray. Nothing looked particularly harmful to a newly
pregnant woman, but then what did he know? Was he
failing his child even now? So soon?

He would remedy that lack of knowledge before
morning, he vowed silently. Hell, he would consume
every report ever written on pregnancy and parenting,
if necess—

'You look…distressed.' Her head tilted to one side
and he couldn't stop his gaze from tracking the smooth
line of her neck, a place he'd thoroughly explored during their night together. A place he yearned to explore
again. 'Is it socially unacceptable to say I hope your
guilt is eating you alive?'

Seve was stunned by his first instinct to laugh. Hell,
he couldn't help cracking a smile, which made her eyes
widen to alluring pools that roused his libido.

'You never have to be circumspect around me,

pequeña. In fact, I would prefer you not to even try. I can handle raw honesty.'

'Can you? You don't believe in practising it yourself.'

His mood soured further and he didn't appreciate the pangs that irritated his insides. 'You need to stop insisting I lied to you. I showed you my true colours. You chose to disregard it. That's on you, not me.'

Her lips pursed and he bit the inside of his cheek to stop him from surging forward, tugging the plump curve into his mouth. She would probably claw his eyes out *and* leave her gouges on his skin if he tried.

So why did that make his blood thicken even more in his veins?

He would definitely have some serious explaining to do to his grandmother if he landed in Cardosia with claw marks on his face. Even more than he anticipated was coming his way.

'What's so funny?' she griped, and he realised, despite his mood, his lips had curved at the thought of what awaited him in Cardosia.

'I'm looking forward to you meeting my grandmother,' he said before he could process the wisdom of it.

'You have family there?' she burst out, the napkin she'd picked up suspended in the air. Then she frowned, possibly because, like his, the statement had slipped out without permission. 'Of course, you do,' she muttered a moment later. 'Do they condone kidnapping too?'

The last of his humour washed away. 'I would rather you don't air our personal business in front of the staff or my grandmother.'

'I think you have *personal business* confused with cross-border crime.'

'You think taking my seed into your body and growing our child in your womb isn't as personal as it gets?'

He'd intended to be earthy enough to remind her of their frenzied coupling, and he knew he'd succeeded when blood rushed into her face. Her eyes grew a little dazed, as if recollecting how they'd got here was as sensually visceral to her as it was to him.

He reached forward, tucked a strand of hair behind her ear, then drifted his knuckle down her heated cheek. 'You wanted a clinical conception. Instead you got a mind-altering experience that is set to change both our lives. No one needs to know the details of how this baby was conceived or how we plan to raise it.'

'We?' The word shook out of her. There was sceptical curiosity in the question, but he didn't blame her. He had a million anxiety-laced questions too.

There was a reason he chose to battle Cardosia's problems from afar. A reason he hadn't come face to face with his uncle for half a decade.

Until now.

Too much hung in the balance. Not least of all his unborn child.

'Oh, yes. We.' He didn't elaborate beyond that. There would be more than enough time to unveil his further plans once they were in Cardosia. 'Eat your meal. Then come join me in the lounge. We land in forty-five minutes.'

Genie ate more out of necessity than appetite.

Sleep had done nothing to calm her roiling nerves. She was still lugging them like unwanted baggage when she set the tray aside and went into the bathroom to refresh herself. Once again she met her gaze in her mirror. This time she looked poleaxed with a peculiar shine to her eyes she couldn't explain.

Shock, maybe? Anticipation of the fight ahead?

Because she wasn't going to just lie down and take Seve's diktat on what the next months of her pregnancy were going to be, was she?

No, she assured herself forcefully when her brain dared to ponder the answer. She hadn't come this far just to hand the reins of her life to someone else.

Not even a man who had such strong possessive feelings about his child? Feelings that if honed right could benefit their chi—?

Dear God, she wasn't making excuses for him, was she? When he'd all but proclaimed her an unfit mother?

She turned around and marched out of the bathroom and suite and down the narrow corridor that led to the main lounge.

Whatever fighting words brewed on her tongue vanished at the sight of him.

He was staring out of the window of the plane, lost in thought. It gave her valuable seconds to examine him unnoticed, although in the next breath she realised her thoughts were severely lacking in value when her senses obsessed over tracing his astounding, almost formidable good looks. With the sun's angle beaming worshipfully on his profile, picking out the dark gold flecks in his brown hair, he was almost too profoundly beautiful.

The strong forehead, the aquiline perfection of his nose and—just as arresting as it'd been weeks ago—the sensually potent curve of his lips all served to deliver a potion kick to her senses.

There was also no value in daydreaming about whether their son—if their child turned out to be male—

would inherit his father's magnetising good looks and overpowering personality, but she found herself doing so anyway. Found herself speculating if, by dallying with this man, she'd saddled herself with a life-long reminder of him in her child.

Of course, you have. This exceptional DNA wouldn't allow for anything less than total domination.

His head swung around, hawk-sharp eyes zeroing in on her with a ferocity that snatched her breath. It said he could read her every thought; knew his impact on her. Probably *revelled* in it.

That real possibility paralysed her for a second before Genie forced herself to move.

To pretend his effect on her wasn't alarming. 'I can't force you to get your pilot to turn this plane around. And for the sake of this pregnancy, I don't intend to zip across time zones with gleeful abandon. I will stay in Cardosia for twenty-four hours only. Anything beyond that and I will report you to the authorities for abduction. Are we clear?' she snapped with, she hoped, enough bite to distract her from noticing everything sinfully attractive about her captor.

But as one corner of his mouth quirked with amusement at her ultimatum, an inner voice was echoing one question across her brain.

Just how do you plan to stop him?

CHAPTER FIVE

TWENTY-FOUR HOURS.

HE HAD NO plans to agree to that, of course.

But it bought him time without anticipating that she would do something foolish, like attempt to throw herself out of the SUV transporting them from the private airport to his estate. Or flee in the middle of the night.

She was extremely wealthy in her own right now, thanks to his purchase, and had the means to vanish if she so wished. Not without a trace, of course, because he simply wouldn't allow that to happen. Not with his child in tow.

But a lot could happen in twenty-four hours. So he curbed his satisfied smile and watched from the corner of his eye as she tried to hide her awe at the surroundings.

Cardosia's beauty was soul-stirring, and it wasn't just because it was the country of his birth. As a young boy, he'd often wondered how cruelty could exist in such a magnificent place. As a man, he knew humanity's brutality needed very little kindling to ignite.

Did such a kindling exist in him?

He pushed the chilling thought away and forced himself to look around too.

Cardosia rivalled its onshore neighbouring Argentina and Chile in dramatic soaring mountains, world-class wineries and thoroughbred horses royalty and billionaires vied for.

But there was one resource that set it apart on the world stage Cardosia's deep, priceless diamond mines. Cardosian diamonds were a rare deep purple not found anywhere else on earth. A resource that turned covetous eyes on his country.

That he had personally had a hand in elevating Cardosia's standing was a source of inner pride. But that pride had been severely dented in the last decade, especially when that exposure had led to exploitation by his uncle, serving only to fatten the older man's greed.

His smile dimmed at the reminder of why he needed to do better before his beloved homeland was decimated economically and ecologically to the point of no return.

Not just for him and his people, but for his unborn child.

She leaned forward to catch another view of yet another striking landmark and he took the opportunity to observe her closer. Her flawless profile. The curve of her breasts. Her flat belly where his child was resting and growing. And every last tinge of guilt melted away.

He was doing the right thing.

At the very least his *abuela* would be happy once he delivered the news. After years of her despairing quietly over him, he was returning with news that would win him mega points.

'Unless you possess X-ray vision, I fail to see why you're staring at my belly.'

His gaze shifted up to meet hers.

Despite her curt tone, her face was flushed and her breathing was a little elevated, no doubt at his blatant scrutiny of her body.

Seve restrained the wanton need prowling through him and shrugged. 'I should warn you to prepare yourself for more of it, *pequeña*. My seed is growing inside you. I find that a singularly primal experience and I won't apologise for revelling in it.'

A light quiver took hold of her bottom lip before she drew it between her teeth, making him stifle a groan. 'I would never have taken you for the primitive type. My research said you're an ultra-modern man who thrives on forward thinking, and yet here you are, talking like a Neanderthal.'

A smile curved his lips, surprising him. 'I'm multidextrous in my thinking. I can be many things without losing who I am. And you really shouldn't believe everything you read online.'

Any response was halted when their SUV drove through the tall Valente-crested iron gates guarding the entrance to his estate. Although she tried to feign boredom, her gaze swung left and right, taking in the tall cypress trees lining the long driveway, and the rolling pastures beyond, and in the far distance the beach where his yacht was moored.

She glanced to her left, her breath catching faintly when she spotted the horses grazing half a kilometre away.

Seve knew that were he to ask in that moment if she loved horses, she would've denied it, just to be contrary. But he made a mental note to introduce her to his favourite stallion.

He watched as she finally looked forward to the sprawling villa that was his favourite place on earth. The home he'd built for his grandmother after years of enforced estrangement by his parents, who'd forbidden his *abuela* from seeing him because she'd had strong views of their shortcomings.

Seve was bitter about a lot of things regarding his childhood, but the deliberate shattering of his relationship with his grandmother would cut deep for ever.

The good thing was she was fully installed in his life now.

He held up a staying hand when his driver alighted and reached for Genie's door. 'Before we go in, there's one thing we need to establish. My grandmother. She's made of stern stuff but I still don't want her to be upset by any of this. Whatever is happening between you and I stays between us. Is that understood?'

Stunning, intelligent eyes regarded him with a hint of smugness. 'You do realise you've just handed me leverage, don't you?'

He allowed himself another smile. 'No, I haven't. Because I did my research too. And I'm fairly confident you don't go around upsetting old ladies just for the fun of it.'

Her long lashes swept down, guarding her expression, but he didn't need to see it to know his assessment was accurate. Of course, she came back fighting. 'Since I'm going to be here barely a day, it shouldn't be a problem. But...' her head tilted imperiously, her eyes narrowing as she stared down her pert nose at him '...misfiring social cues or not, I won't lie or cover up for what you're doing. If you're in hot water with your grandmother, you're there of your own making.'

Amusement and attraction for this little lioness swelled within him. He nodded at the driver to open the door before he did something foolish, like drag her into his lap and devour those Snow White lips. 'Warning duly noted.'

He watched her alight, her long, shapely legs outlined in the dress flattened to her body by the light breeze. When she lifted her hand to tuck away a curl disturbed by the same breeze, Seve swallowed a groan. He needed to keep his head in the game, not salivate over her like some hormonal teenager.

The towering front doors opening behind Genie helped him put aside the need rampaging through him. His grandmother rushed out, curiosity snapping in her dark brown eyes as she reached the top of the steps.

'Severino! I was only informed of your arrival a few hours ago. Why didn't you tell me you planned to come home?' she snapped, but the warmth in her eyes belied her tone, soothing some of the ruffles inside him.

Going to her, he caught the hands she held out and kissed the soft, lined cheek she tilted towards him. 'My plans changed unexpectedly,' was all he said.

Her lips pursed but her gaze darted past him. 'And you've brought a guest, I see?'

He turned to where Genie stood, her fingers clasped demurely before her. '*Sí*. This is Genie Merchant. Genie, meet my grandmother, Julieta Valente.'

The two women eyed each other for a long second before Genie held out her hand. 'A pleasure to meet you, Señora Valente.'

His grandmother immediately waved her away. 'I don't respond to "Señora Valente", child. Everyone calls me Lita, short for *abuelita*. And so will you.'

Genie looked startled for a moment, then she frowned before her gaze darted to his. At his nod, she glanced back at his grandmother. 'I will.' And after a moment, 'Thank you,' she tagged on.

The old woman smiled. '*Buena*. Now come, get out of the sun. I have refreshments ready in the *salon*.'

For a moment, Genie wanted to protest.

To remind the man walking beside her with his arm tucked courteously around his grandmother's that she wasn't here for a social visit.

But she'd granted him twenty-four hours.

For her baby's sake, those hours included rest and sustenance. And, as Seve had annoyingly and accurately pointed out, she wasn't in the business of upsetting old ladies. And his grandmother was as darling as they came.

The diminutive woman packed a punch but every glance she cast her grandson was filled with warmth. The kind Genie hadn't experienced in a very long time, if ever. So she bit her tongue and accompanied them down a gorgeous, warmly lit corridor, decorated on either side with art and artefacts bearing heavy South American influences. It was clear Seve took pride in his Cardosian home with the sheer number of renowned artists' work that graced his walls.

Despite his wealthy status there was no Rembrandt or Monet flouting his prestige, just golden-hued tones that made one room flow into the other, ending in a sunlit salon where a veritable spread awaited them on a sleek table set to one side of the room.

A buxom woman introduced as Sofia, the house-keeper, waited alongside a butler. The two older women exchanged a few murmured words before she hurried off.

Lita took a seat in a wide rocking armchair that looked out of place in the opulent room.

'Help yourself to some grilled shrimp, Genie. Sofia uses a dash of Cardosian spices that are simply heavenly. And serve your guest some Cardosian wine, *cariño*. We make the best reds in the world,' she boasted with a pride-filled smile.

Genie opened her mouth but Seve beat her to it. 'Genie can't take wine, Lita. Or shellfish.'

Lita's eyes widened, then her face started to fall before the coin dropped. '*Santa María*, that can only mean…' Her gaze darted from Genie to Seve. A look passed between them before she clasped her hands over her heart. '*Sí?*'

'*Sí*, Lita,' he confirmed with deep, solemn tones, his face betraying nothing but the news. 'Genie is carrying my child. You're going to be a great-grandmother in a little under seven months.'

The old lady jumped from her seat, completely belying her age by rushing forward to engulf Seve in a hug. He leaned down and allowed himself to be kissed on both cheeks.

And then Lita turned to Genie. Her effusiveness was a touch reduced but her smile was no less warm. 'You've made an old woman very happy, *carina*,' she said in accented English.

Genie opened her mouth to speak but, a little terrified she would say the wrong thing, shut it again and merely nodded.

Lita bustled over to the table, waving the butler away when he stepped forward. Muttering excitedly under her breath, she heaped a plate full of heavenly smelling food and hurried over to Genie. 'You must eat, child. Valente mothers make fat, beautiful babies but we can't rely on just nature to get the job done.'

The image of herself with a swollen belly months from now made Genie's breath catch. Filled her with such overwhelming feelings she could only nod again and accept the plate of food. Studying it, she noticed that Lita had picked everything a pregnant woman could safely eat.

And surprisingly, her appetite was ready for the delicate pastries, the stuffed peppers and vegetable kebabs making her mouth water.

She was mostly ignored as Lita chattered excitedly to her grandson.

But when the room fell silent, she glanced up to see two sets of eyes on her. Lita's dropped fleetingly to Genie's left hand, a hint of a question in her eyes before Seve rose to his feet.

'Give her time to adjust. This is all news to Genie too.'

Lita frowned. 'News to her? But you said she's two—'

'I know what I said, Lita,' Seve interrupted firmly, faint warning in his tone making the old woman's lips purse. 'The priority for Genie now is to get some rest. We crossed several time zones to get here.'

'But we will have dinner together tonight, *si*?' Lita pressed.

'If Genie is up to it, yes.' He reached her and glanced at her nearly finished plate. 'Are you ready to be shown to your room?'

A chance to be alone? To take all this in?

Hell, yes.

Setting the plate aside, she rose.

Lita approached them with a smile. 'Are you sure you've had enough? I can have another plate brought up to your room?'

Seve glanced sternly at his grandmother. 'You need to eat too, and rest.'

She made a face and waved him away. 'I'm only seventy-five, not a hundred and five. Besides, I can sleep when I'm dead.'

'Technically, being dead isn't sleeping. It's ceasing to exist,' Genie retorted.

Lita looked startled for a moment, then she threw her head back and laughed.

Genie looked bewildered. Adorably so. So much so Seve wanted to run his knuckle down her flushing skin.

He locked his knees and frowned at himself.

Since when was he obsessed with finding excuses to touch a woman? Normally, the reverse was what occurred. Except in this moment, he couldn't think of any other woman he wanted to touch more than the one staring at his beloved grandmother as if she were a cipher she dearly wanted to decode.

'I like this one. But I get the feeling she doesn't like you very much,' Lita said to him.

'I don't,' Genie responded in perfect Cardosian, making his grandmother's eyes sparkle even brighter in pleasure as she smiled wider in delight.

'You speak Cardosian?' she asked, approval brimming in her voice.

Genie nodded briskly. 'I do, and if you want to know why I don't like him, your grandson—'

'Would like nothing more than to get himself and his guest settled. So shall we?' The warning tone in his voice was hard to miss. By both women. As much as he loved his grandmother, he didn't owe her an explanation for why he'd turned up with a pregnant stranger who was carrying his baby.

As for Genie…

She got the hint well enough to purse her lips as the housekeeper stepped forward and ushered her out.

His grandmother watched everything with shrewd eyes, and when he caught her gaze, she raised an eyebrow. He shook his head, prompting the old woman to stay her words once more.

Genie eyed him the moment they stepped into the corridor.

'You two always speak to each other in sign language?'

'When you know each other that well, it helps. Who knows, you and I might develop a unique language of our own.'

A blush flew up to envelop her cheeks, but, of course, her eyes remained rapier sharp with displeasure. 'I wouldn't hold my breath if I were you.'

He stepped close enough to say his next words directly into her ear so they wouldn't be overheard. 'But there could be fun in that. There's a reason erotic asphyxiation exists, *pequeña*.'

He caught her elbow as she stumbled over her feet. Her blush bloomed into a full-blown flush he wanted to explore with his hands. Then his lips.

'You…you're outrageous. I would never indulge in such…proclivities!'

His gaze traced her graceful, voluptuous body, lingering on where his seed was growing, where his baby would bask for the next several months. Something about that earthly, primal knowledge only served to heighten the arousal that lurked so close to the surface when he was near her. 'Not in your current state, obviously, but who knows what will happen in the future, hmm?'

'Nothing remotely like that you…you pig!'

'Don't knock it until you try it. Remember how good it was between us? Tell me you had anything even close to that and I'll call you a liar,' he challenged.

Her nostrils flared but Seve, with every sinew strained towards this woman who fascinated him more than any other creature on the planet, also noticed that her eyes sparkled in that thirsty, experience-seeking way they had before.

'One experience, no matter how…noteworthy, doesn't mean I'm all in to throw myself over the edge of a cliff, Mr Valente.'

'Seve,' he insisted. Then when he caught a glimpse of her mutiny on this small issue too, he changed tack. 'Or you can call me Mr Valente. But know that that will trigger even more evocative scenarios of me disciplining you in the most deliciously decadent possible way.'

She gasped once more, further outrage bristling through her frame. But her nipples still puckered, her chest rising and falling in sweet, tormenting agitation. 'You really are a Neanderthal, aren't you?'

He smiled. 'You're outraged, maybe even genuinely, but it's not stopping you from being extremely interested in the possibilities. Your heartbeat is elevated and your pupils are dilated. I may not be a scientist but I'm well versed in body language.'

She shrugged. 'That doesn't mean anything. Human beings are programmed to learn through experiences but that's not to say I want to dip my hand into a fire just to see how hot it burns.'

He realised his fingers were caressing the velvet-soft skin of her arm. For the life of him he couldn't bring himself to stop. 'Oh, yes, you do. You thrive on it.'

Her lips parted on a scathing put-down, but then her eyes widened as she accepted the unvarnished truth. But a blink later and she was scrambling for composure. 'Not enough to do…that with you, I assure you. In fact, I would be obliged if you took your hand off me.'

Reluctantly, Seve dropped his hand, and resumed walking down the hallway. From the corner of his eye he saw her flit him a glance and he curbed a smile. As unexpected as it'd been, he'd enjoyed yet another skirmish he hadn't even consciously instigated.

Their brief history had taught him that Genie drove a hard bargain. Always. And he was beginning to relish every fight with her.

The next months would be nothing if not entertaining.

What on earth was wrong with her?

He'd mentioned sex—the serious risqué kind she imagined only took place in dungeons and racy BDSM clubs—and she'd immediately gone up in flames. Had shockingly imagined it for a nanosecond before fleeing from the thought.

She was pregnant, for heaven's sake!

Being pregnant doesn't mean sex—of any kind—is off the table…

She exhaled in exasperation as the housekeeper,

who'd patiently waited a discreet distance away while Seve had rumbled on about his insane proclivities, nudged open elegant double doors and stood to one side with a gentle smile.

Genie stepped through the doors and her senses were engulfed by a different kind of overwhelming.

It was starkly different from the room she'd called her bedroom in her building for the better part of a decade. This was…magically beautiful.

Soft dove grey blended with the barest hint of blush accents, right down to the grey and blush carpet, the same colour theme on the art and decor gracing the room. Even the bedding carried on the scheme, although the pillows and covers held more blush pink than grey.

Genie had the most peculiar urge to run her fingers over everything, feel the textures beneath her fingertips. Let some of the calm tranquillity seep into her soul. She gave in, her senses settling a little when the inviting coolness made her sigh.

Of course, all of that calmness evaporated when she looked up to find Seve watching her, his gaze moving from her face to her fingers and back again.

Sofia murmuring that her things had been unpacked and pointing to the adjoining dressing room thankfully disrupted the sure path to further agitation.

A nod from Seve and the housekeeper left the room. When his gaze dropped back to her hand, now clutching a clump of bedspread, she refused to react.

'Get some rest, *pequeña*. Your personal maid will be on standby to draw you a bath if you require. We will speak further later.'

'I fail to see what about. I'm leaving in—'

'T minus twenty-one hours. Yes, I'm aware you're

counting down. But until the time is up, you'll indulge me. *Si?*'

He was walking away before she even responded, as if her answer didn't matter. As if his mind was already made up. Weariness and the need to avoid another verbal skirmish—although thus far each one with Seve had been absurdly stimulating—made her bite her tongue.

And berate herself when she got her wish to be alone and immediately wanted him back. Wished back that invigorating force field that reminded her with every second that she was *alive*.

She sagged against the bed, let out a long exhale and kicked off her shoes. She wanted a shower. Needed to gather her thoughts. Contact the contractors who'd been expecting her in Norway to tell them she'd been unexpectedly delayed.

But weariness was dragging down every cell in her body.

And the bed was *so* inviting.

So she gave in, crawled under the sheets, and let sleep take her.

'He's a Cardosian Blanco.'

'Indeed.'

Seve watched as Genie ran her hand down the stallion's forehead and felt something intensely needful kick in his groin. She'd found him in his study after a two-hour nap and—from the scent of shampoo and alluring perfume torturing his senses—a bath. Her hair was coiled in a loose knot atop her head, leaving the elegant line of her neck to his full view.

He'd made the wise choice to start the tour outside so Lita wouldn't bombard Genie with the questions she'd

"One Minute" Survey

You get up to **FOUR books** <u>and</u> a Mystery Gift...

> **ABSOLUTELY FREE!**

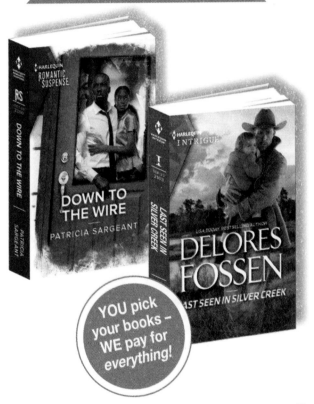

> YOU pick your books – WE pay for everything!

See inside for details.

YOU pick your books –
WE pay for everything.
You got up to **FOUR** new books and a Mystery Gift...
absolutely FREE!
Total retail value: Over $20!

Dear Reader,

Your opinions are important to us. So if you'll participate in our fast and free "One Minute" Survey, YOU can pick up to four wonderful books that WE pay for when you try the Harlequin Reader Service!

As a leading publisher of women's fiction, we'd love to hear from you. That's why we promise to reward you for completing our survey.

IMPORTANT: Please complete the survey and return it. We'll send your Free Books and a Free Mystery Gift right away. And we pay for shipping and handling too!

← *We pay for EVERYTHING!*

Try **Harlequin® Romantic Suspense** and get 2 books featuring heart-racing page-turners with unexpected plot twists and irresistible chemistry that will keep you guessing to the very end.

Try **Harlequin Intrigue® Larger-Print** and get 2 books featuring action-packed stories that will keep you on the edge of your seat. Solve the crime and deliver justice at all costs.

Or TRY BOTH!

Thank you again for participating in our "One Minute" Survey. It really takes just a minute (or less) to complete the survey... and your free books and gift will be well worth it!

If you continue with your subscription, you can look forward to curated monthly shipments of brand-new books from your selected series, always at a discount off the cover price! Plus you can cancel any time. So don't miss out, return your One Minute Survey today to get your Free books.

Pam Powers

"One Minute" Survey

GET YOUR FREE BOOKS AND A FREE GIFT!

✓ Complete this Survey   ✓ Return this survey

▼ DETACH AND MAIL CARD TODAY! ▼

1 Do you try to find time to read every day?

☐ YES   ☐ NO

2 Do you prefer stories with suspenseful storylines?

☐ YES   ☐ NO

3 Do you enjoy having books delivered to your home?

☐ YES   ☐ NO

4 Do you share your favorite books with friends?

☐ YES   ☐ NO

YES! I have completed the above "One Minute" Survey. Please send me my Free Books and a Free Mystery Gift (worth over $20 retail). I understand that I am under no obligation to buy anything, as explained on the back of this card.

☐ **Harlequin® Romantic Suspense**
240/340 CTI G2AD

☐ **Harlequin Intrigue® Larger-Print**
199/399 CTI G2AD

☐ **BOTH**
240/340 & 199/399 CTI G2AE

FIRST NAME

LAST NAME

ADDRESS

APT.#

CITY

STATE/PROV.

ZIP/POSTAL CODE

EMAIL ☐ Please check this box if you would like to receive newsletters and promotional emails from Harlequin Enterprises ULC and its affiliates. You can unsubscribe anytime.

© 2023 HARLEQUIN ENTERPRISES ULC
™ and ® are trademarks owned by Harlequin Enterprises ULC. Printed in the U.S.A.

HI/HRS-1123-OM

✿ HARLEQUIN® Reader Service —**Here's how it works:**

Accepting your 2 free books and free gift (gift valued at approximately $10.00 retail) places you under no obligation to buy anything. You may keep the books and gift and return the shipping statement marked "cancel." If you do not cancel, approximately one month later we'll send you more books from the series you have chosen, and bill you at our low, subscribers-only discount price. Harlequin® Romantic Suspense books consist of 4 books each month and cost just $5.99 each in the U.S. or $6.74 each in Canada, a savings of at least 8% off the cover price. Harlequin Intrigue® Larger-Print books consist of 6 books each month and cost just $6.99 each in the U.S. or $7.49 each in Canada, a savings of at least 10% off the cover price. It's quite a bargain! Shipping and handling is just 50¢ per book in the U.S. and $1.25 per book in Canada. You may return any shipment at our expense and cancel at any time by contacting customer service — or you may continue to receive monthly shipments at our low, subscribers-only discount price plus shipping and handling.

▼ If offer card is missing write to: Harlequin Reader Service, P.O. Box 1341, Buffalo, NY 14240-8531 or visit www.ReaderService.com ▼

BUSINESS REPLY MAIL
FIRST-CLASS MAIL   PERMIT NO. 717   BUFFALO, NY

POSTAGE WILL BE PAID BY ADDRESSEE

HARLEQUIN READER SERVICE
PO BOX 1341
BUFFALO NY 14240-8571

NO POSTAGE
NECESSARY
IF MAILED
IN THE
UNITED STATES

fired at Seve for a full hour before he'd taken refuge in his study.

Of course, he hadn't taken into account that Genie would enthral his favourite stallion, too.

'What's his name?' she asked.

'Cyclone, so named for his terrible temperament before he learned the error of his ways.'

She hummed under her breath as she caressed him, her gaze moving over the other six horses in the paddock.

'They're breathtaking. *You're* breathtaking,' she whispered to the horse, a world removed from the woman who'd laid down the law on the plane a few short hours ago. The woman who had fought him with words every single step.

Like everything about her, her many facets intrigued him far too much. And yet he couldn't draw his gaze away from her fingers, from the soft wonder on her face as she caressed the horse.

His horse. Which he was in danger of feeling peevishly jealous of.

'You'll have to admire them from afar for the time being, I'm afraid.'

A layer of softness receded when she glanced at him. 'You mean in the…' she glanced pointedly at her watch '…eighteen hours and nineteen minutes I'm here.'

He shrugged. 'If it pleases you to keep reminding me of the ticking clock, sure.'

Her hand slowly dropped from Cyclone's muzzle, a thing that didn't please the stallion, who attempted to nudge her touch back. And wasn't it a hell of a thing to now feel a kinship with his horse?

'I'm getting the impression that you're simply humouring my intention to leave tomorrow.'

'And there I thought I was giving you a tour.'

'I've seen your stables, your beach, your swimming pool and the admirable recycling project you've got going. I know your estate runs on an eco-safe fuel system. I would've thought a man of your position would have better things to do than devote so much time escorting me around his home.'

His jaw clenched. 'You keep making the mistake of not taking me at my word. I said you and the baby you're carrying are now my priority. You will do well to start believing me.'

'But what has it got to do with all this?' She gestured to the paddock and the stables beyond. 'Unless...' Wariness crept into her eyes. 'Unless you're humouring me because you don't intend to let me leave?'

He turned from her, striding to the electric buggy they'd used for their tour. 'Get in, Genie. We'll talk inside.'

From the corner of his eye, he watched her hesitate, then walk to the vehicle.

She remained silent for a full minute before sending a searing glance his way. 'You can't keep me here. I have plans for my future that don't include...whatever it is you've got up your sleeve for me.'

Seve nodded. 'You'll have a chance to tell me what those plans are when we get inside.'

He sensed her surprise, then her wariness. 'Is this a trick?'

'I promised you a discussion when you woke up. We're going to have it now.'

Minutes later, he watched her march into his study

as if she owned the room. And, hell, if he wasn't capti-vated by her fighting spirit. When she went to speak, he stopped her. Crossing the room, he poured her a glass of blended juice Lita had sent Sofia with when she saw them returning. No doubt his grandmother would be monitoring Genie's food and drink intake with the fer-vour of a brooding hen.

'Drink this or Lita will have both our heads.'

She accepted the glass from him, her breathing wa-vering a little when their fingers touched. She took a sip, no doubt to be polite, then, eyes widening a fraction at the delicious taste, she gulped down the refreshing juice. A little self-consciously, she licked her lips and set the glass down.

'These plans of yours. Tell me about them,' he said.

'Bring me a laptop and I will.'

He crossed the room and returned with a sleek, brand-new device. Taking a seat next to her on the wide sofa, he watched her fingers fly across the keys with mesmerising efficiency. Ninety seconds later, she turned the screen to him.

It showed a sizeable piece of land about the size of his west paddock. In the pages that followed were elaborate plans of her intentions for the land. The more he read, the more the mixture of pride and fury stirred faster through him. Perhaps he was searching for a conclusive excuse, one she'd just handed him on a platter. But he took it and let it erode the last of his guilt.

'Everything on there is self-sustaining. Even the electricity.' Her tone was prideful. A touch defensive.

'You planned all of this?' he asked, even though he knew she did.

'Yes. It's been a year in the planning. The only thing

keeping me from making it a reality is this imposed prison sentence.'

'Impressive. Your plan for one hundred per cent sustainability is highly commendable. But it's still not good enough. You're yet to put this all together and it's not advisable to take on such a project in your condition. Besides, it's too isolated. There are no medical facilities for hundreds of miles. What if something happens to you or the baby?'

She gritted her teeth. 'I had contingencies in place for that.'

'You don't need to have them here. You're surrounded by staff, some of whom have medical experience. And a doctor can be summoned within minutes. All that aside, our goals might just align in theory if not geographically.'

Against her will, curiosity bit her. 'What do you mean?'

He didn't answer immediately. Instead, he went to the laptop he'd been using on the plane and activated it. A few clicks later, he turned it towards her.

The file was detailed, with long pages of enticing offers that made her eyes widen.

Doctor's appointments, an elaborate diet plan she could approve or alter at her whim, a workspace of her choice. Yoga or Pilates instructors to attend her in person or remotely, the use of his Olympic-size swimming pool any time she wished. In fact, the whole estate was at her disposal. She would want for nothing and she could work as much or as little as she chose.

In essence, it was eerily similar to the plans she'd made for herself, the only difference being the location.

And her freedom. 'It's my turn to ask if *you* planned all this all along.'

He answered without an ounce of guilt. 'Oh, yes. Everything down to the last detail. While you've been counting down the time until you leave to become an eco-warrior while pregnant with my child, I turned my life inside out. Not for me but for the baby. And therefore for you. You're the vessel keeping him warm and healthy. For now, you're important too. And this is the best place for you to remain. Nothing you've shown me convinces me otherwise.'

For now.

He couldn't have spelled out more explicitly how expendable she'd eventually come to be to him if he'd tried.

'Except it's not what I want,' she said. Then watched as his eyes gleamed with the fire of determination that announced that he was about to bring out the big guns.

'You see me letting you go as the only viable solution when I've presented you with several ways we could make this work,' he drawled. Whether he kept his voice low because it was a prelude to pouncing or not was neither here nor there.

It affected Genie as strongly in sending tremors through her body.

'None so far that are good enough. Name another.'

He paused for a fraction of a second. Then laid down his final card.

'Marry me.'

CHAPTER SIX

GENIE FELT HER eyes blink in comical slow motion.

Once. Twice. Then twice more. 'What?' The word gushed like a chain-smoking screen siren's whisper. Equally comical. She just couldn't seem to make her voice work properly.

'Marry me. Be my wife. Join me in full parenting of our child.'

She blinked again, her nostrils fluttering with emotions too illogical to name. And because she feared she couldn't contain them one second longer, she expelled them in a firm, 'No.'

The billionaire venture capitalist who'd dated some of the world's most beautiful women obviously wasn't used to being denied.

Seve's eyed widened. Not as comically as hers had, she imagined. But still, there was distinct surprise, then a tensing. As if a sucker punch to his gut had winded him.

Not that he let it show for long. 'Why not?'

Why not?

There was no need to beat about the bush. Hell, she wanted to lay it all out there in the hope that this unnerving sensation would dissipate by exposure. 'Because I don't like the way your proposal makes my insides feel.'

Something wicked and dangerous gleamed in his eyes. 'Describe it. In detail.'

'Unnerved. Elated. Then deflated. I think the common term is roller-coaster emotions. And they are a sign of weakness. For the sake of this child, I can't be weak.' There. That was plain and stark enough.

His eyes glinted even more, pure relish entering the dark depths. 'Or it's a sign that you simply need time to let it settle, to get used to the idea.'

'Why? It'll change nothing.'

He shrugged. 'It'll give you time for clearer thinking. Roller coasters don't go on for ever. When they end, it's the abiding feeling that remains that is the most important. You're describing feelings based here…' he trailed his fingers between her breasts, then below over her swollen stomach '…rather than here.' Now his fingers caressed her temple.

Her skin reacted predictably. Chasing the chemical sensation his touch triggered. Then further plummeting her emotions when he dropped his hand.

It wasn't productive or wise to keep chasing that reaction.

And yet…she couldn't think of a counterargument, especially not when his sensual lips were moving again, forming words she needed to concentrate on.

'But should you require a little of the roller-coaster effect, we can have that too.'

'But that's…illogical. I just said it was counterproductive.'

'Not everything needs to be experienced in those

terms, *pequeña*, A second helping of ice cream is sinful, but you do it anyway.'

'Just so we're clear, is ice cream a euphemism for sex?' she blurted, then continued to hold his gaze, even as her face flamed.

'I don't need to hide behind euphemisms. Marry me. Agree to joint custody and live in Cardosia. Have sex with me if that's the roller coaster you want to jump on. We both know you enjoy sex with me. And when that inevitably wanes, we'll devote ourselves to our child's upbringing.'

The purest strain of wicked temptation shivered through her before she pushed it firmly away. 'No. This wasn't part of my plan. I don't need a man to be the best parent I can be for my child. Nor do I need sex.'

His jaw tightened and his eyes narrowed into formidable slits. Genie expected him to breathe fire next, as anatomically impossible as that was. But then he'd shown her that there was far more to human interaction than just words and actions. There were…feelings. Indescribable sensations. Yearning as powerful and palpable as loneliness.

'Plans change,' he said eventually. 'You didn't plan on selling your algorithm to me and yet you did because I presented the best outcome you needed.'

'You're not comparing an algorithm to a child, are you?'

'You enjoy reducing everything to logic. I'm putting it in terms we can both work with.'

She opened her mouth to debate that, but he held up his hand. The gesture made her bristle, even as his elegant fingers evoked memories of how they'd felt just now on her body.

Seriously, what was wrong with her?

'Take the rest of your hours to decide, *pequeña*. Let that clever brain of yours weigh the pros and cons of having a two-parent support system.'

'I've already told you I had two parents who claimed to do their best. That logic is flawed.'

'They claimed it without putting in the work. Will you put in the work?'

She didn't need to think about it for even a nanosecond. 'Of course, I will.'

'So will I. You made the mistake of assuming the father of your child wouldn't want to be involved in your decisions. You need to readjust that thinking. Then go further and explore the logic and advantage of doing it together rather than apart.'

'My original plan was to go a different route.'

His eyes narrowed and Genie got the feeling he wasn't pleased about that. Why did that send such a decadent thrill through her? Was she a closet masochist too? She swallowed, a little perturbed by these layers of herself she was uncovering. What would she discover next? That she craved more of those little terms of Cardosian endearments he tossed at her with seemingly effortless ease?

No. She didn't.

'Then you shouldn't have planted that thought in my head, then taken me into your body so enthusiastically, should you?' he rasped with sizzling conceit.

'Are you blaming me for the protection failing?'

He shrugged. 'It doesn't matter how it happened. It happened.'

And now you're here. You're mine, his ferocious gaze seemed to growl.

'We're getting nowhere,'

'No. We're getting exactly where we need to get to. You're just being stubborn about seeing the merits of it. But you have a little time—'

'Sixteen hours and fifty-seven minutes isn't enough time to consider changing every single plan I have for you.'

'You wound me, *querida*,' he said, although he appeared the least wounded person she'd ever seen. 'Most women I know would jump at the chance to put a ring on me.'

'I'm not most women,' she pointed out, just because she felt a vital need to.

Only to draw an even more devastating smile. One she felt all the way to the last nerve in her small toe. 'I'm bracingly aware of that, Genie.'

And yes, there went another traitorous shiver.

One she cursed herself for reliving in the hours that followed, long after their discussion had ended, and she was hiding away in her room with her laptop.

Dinner was a stilted affair, which seemed to bewilder Lita into filling the silence with chatter, to which her grandson responded with near monosyllabic grunts.

Genie was too frazzled to parse through which social cues she needed to observe to engage with them, so she kept mostly silent, cringing a little inside every time the old woman sent a furtive glance her way, then blamed Seve under her breath for their guest's joylessness.

It would've been almost endearing to see the interaction between grandmother and grandson…if she weren't still reeling from the sharp right turn of Seve's proposal.

As night fell over the estate, the sound of cicadas

and the pine-scented breeze through the open doors leading to the terrace outside the dining room calmed her a touch.

Still, she couldn't wait to escape, and the moment she was done with the heavenly slice of *chocotorta* drizzled with warm honey, she placed her napkin on the table.

'It's been a long day. I think I'll head off to bed.'

For a moment, Seve's jaw clenched but he stood and came around the table to hold her chair, an almost outdated courtesy that nevertheless made her feel that same strange roller-coaster sensation in her belly. Not to mention the effect of his aftershave with him so close.

'Before you go…'

She paused in the doorway, partly glad he'd halted her exit. She wasn't looking forward to spending hours with her thoughts spinning around in circles. And, she suspected, not even the usual thrill of coding would grab her attention.

She turned to face Seve, who'd crossed the room to lean against the giant stone-hewn mantel, one ankle crossed casually over the other. 'The doctor is coming in the morning for a check-up. Unless you have a particular objection?'

Her first check-up as an expectant mother. With the father of her child in attendance. Not how she'd expected any of this to unravel. But she could hardly say no, could she?

Her hand trailed to her stomach, the thought of seeing her baby for the first time, if only in sonogram, a touch overwhelming. 'Not at all.'

It wasn't until his shoulders relaxed fractionally that she realised he'd been tense awaiting her answer. Perhaps thought she might object.

Because that was all she'd done so far, wasn't it? She stiffened at the censorious voice.

'Good. Sleep well, *querida*.'

Another casual, terribly affecting endearment, which sizzled right through her.

Which made his grandmother produce a small, indulgent smile as she added her own goodnight wishes

Genie nodded and fled. Then spent the better part of the night tossing and turning. Her mind whirling back to Seve Valente. And his proposal.

She woke at the crack of dawn no closer to escaping her churning thoughts. In a bid to quiet them, she grabbed her laptop and, going out onto the stunning terrace, lost herself in writing code until the sun kissed the horizon.

When birdsong replaced the chirping of cicadas and sunshine beamed down on her face in warming welcome, her fingers slowed on the keyboard.

Around her the estate was coming to life and, for the first time ever, Genie felt the all-encompassing loneliness recede a touch. Distant laughter and horses neighing lured her to the low wall. She leaned on it, taking in the sights and sounds of the estate.

It was breathtaking…for a prison?

No. She had several hours left before she found out if Seve would truly let her go or if, indeed, he was humouring her. Several hours she could use to progress her initial plans in Norway.

And yet she lingered, breathing in the incredible air and basking in the South American sun. Several minutes later, when she realised she didn't want to move from the perfect spot, Genie forced herself to do just that.

She couldn't afford to get attached to Seve or his beautiful home.

Back inside she took a shower, attempting to ignore the way her senses leapt and shimmered in anticipation the closer the breakfast hour approached. The clothes she'd packed for a temperate Norwegian summer were just as good for what passed for a Cardosian winter, so she dressed in a wispy light cotton shamrock-green sundress and a pair of flat mules and left her hair flowing free. Smoothing on a sun-blocking moisturiser, she grabbed her mobile phone and left the room.

To find Seve stepping out of his own suite halfway down the corridor.

His unapologetic stare made the already excitable butterflies flutter even more frenziedly, and, for the life of her, Genie couldn't stop scrutinising him as intently as he was watching her.

God, it was almost as if it was a silent competition to see who could stare the longest.

Her breath caught when he sauntered towards her. *'Buenos días, pequeña. Dormiste bien?'*

'Realmente, no,' she replied, before it dawned on her that she'd responded in his mother tongue. There was no taking it back.

Nor was there stopping that smug glint in his eyes or the whisper of amusement curving his lips as he stopped before her. 'You should've come to find me. We would've found a cure for your restlessness together.'

'There was no need. I knew exactly what caused it.'

Her accusation bounced off his white linen-shirted shoulders. Combined with the loose palazzo pants, he looked the picture of indolent virility and she was irritated by the effort it took to drag her gaze from his

chiselled jaw and bronzed perfection. For the way her
fingers itched to comb back the damp lock of hair kiss-
ing his forehead.

'The doctor will be here in an hour. Hopefully by
that time, breakfast and a walk in the sun would have
put you in a better disposition?'

She wanted to say there was nothing wrong with
her disposition. But he was holding out his arm and her
brain was short-circuiting at the thought of the sustained
stimulation of their skin touching.

Get yourself together, Genie.

Sucking in a breath, she took his proffered arm.

A few minutes later, they were stepping outside onto
the wide terrace on the opposite side of where they'd
dined last night. The early morning sunlight bathed the
space and a smiling Lita was already seated at the table.

She waved Genie to a seat after accepting a kiss from
her grandson. The conversation was light and general,
a vast difference from last night, much to Genie's relief. She helped herself to fruit, muesli and tea, then, at
Lita's nudging, a helping of warm, buttered bread baked
fresh by Sofia. She was enjoying her second cup of tea
when Lita glanced over at her.

'You're still so pale, child. Don't worry. In no time at
all, that pale skin will be glowing. The little *niño* will
love it too, you'll see.'

Genie's reaction was visceral and immediate. 'But
I'm not staying.'

Lita's eyes widened with confusion, then slowly
darkened with distress. Her gaze shifted to her grandson. As did Genie's.

His earlier congeniality was gone. He was watching
Genie with a chilled message in his eyes.

Don't upset her, it warned.

As recently as yesterday, she would've ignored him. Stated exactly what was on her mind. But Lita had welcomed her with nothing but warmth. It wasn't her fault that her grandson was a Neanderthal who went around kidnapping women to his gorgeous South American estate.

Not women. Just you.

And it was probably in that moment, when outrage should've been her reigning emotion but instead there deigned to be a swelling for this special exclusivity, that Genie realised she was dangerously close to losing her way. To buckling under Seve Valente's demands.

'What does she mean?' Lita asked her grandson.

Seve's jaw gritted. 'Nothing for you to worry about, Lita.'

The old woman glared at him. 'I'll be the judge of what I need to worry about, *mijo*.' She turned to Genie, skewering her with a look so much like her grandson's, Genie's breath caught. 'Are you planning to leave?' There was mild accusation in her tone. And, absurdly, guilt stung Genie.

She glanced at Seve, but he wasn't inclined to save her now she'd upset his precious grandmother and placed herself in the old woman's crosshairs.

Genie licked her lips as he reached for the carafe of orange juice, poured her a glass and proceeded to pour himself some heavenly smelling coffee.

He took his time to sip it, his eyes mocking her over the top of the expensive china.

'I had…have a project that I'm working on that I need to return to.'

'Do you?' Seve enquired with deceptive mildness.

'Yes,' she insisted, struggling not to scowl.

'Perhaps you should double-check those plans before you make hasty decisions?'

A chill washed over her neck. 'What are you talking about?'

He shrugged but before she could push for an answer, the butler stepped onto the terrace. '*Señor*, the doctor and his team are here.'

A different sort of tension swept over the table. The only one who looked excited was Lita. Seve pinned Genie with a look as he came around to grip the back of her chair. Under the guise of helping her up, he murmured in her ear, 'We'll pick this up later.'

'We most certainly will.'

Their march back indoors was far more strained than when they'd come down half an hour ago. Genie kicked herself for feeling bereft for it. And even as she was introduced to the middle-aged female doctor with her all-female crew, something churned in her chest that closely resembled desolation.

The portable gurney set up in one of the smaller sitting rooms was comfortable, yet Genie couldn't bring herself to relax. The series of questions Dr Dominici asked her didn't help, conscious as Genie was of Seve's domineering presence beside her.

As one of the doctor's team made notes on a tablet, Genie felt fingers caressing her temple. 'Relax, *pequeña*. All this tension isn't good for the baby.'

The words were low and evenly spoken against her ear, but they held the tiniest edge that did the opposite. Seve felt it, and she sensed his displeasure as he straightened again. But in the next moment, her belly was being exposed by Dr Dominici, and Seve's fin-

gers were wrapping around hers as the screen flick-
ered to life.

And then an alarming thing happened.

Awe filled her as she saw the bundle of cells that
was her baby for the first time, just as Seve's fingers
brushed soothingly over her knuckles, making her spine
ease against the bed and the tension ooze right out of
her. Genie couldn't have separated the two emotions if
her life depended on it. And when strong hands tightened around hers, she tightened hers in return. She told
herself she couldn't look away from the screen because
she didn't want to miss a thing.

But deep down she knew she wasn't ready to see the
same emotions weaving through her reflected in Seve's
face. Or worse…*not*.

And weren't pregnancy emotions truly the worst?
Because now her jumbled emotions were making her
eyes prickle and the blood rush into her ears, and the
insidious voice asking if she was truly ready to go off
to Norway, continue this journey on her own when she
could stay right here. In the sun and warmth and mercurial but, oh, so stimulating presence of her infuriating captor.

A peculiar sound escaped her throat before she could
stop it. More alarming reaction to add to the suddenly
mystifying code that was her life.

'Everything all right?' Dr Dominici asked.

Genie cleared her throat. 'I believe I…we should be
asking you that.'

The doctor smiled. '*Sí*. Everything is as it should be.
The heartbeat is strong and the measurements show
you're almost ten weeks along. We will be able to tell
the sex of the baby on the next scan if you're interested?'

Genie felt Seve's gaze boring into her, compelling hers. Unable to resist, she glanced up at him. And there it was. The formidably powerful range of emotions she'd been too terrified to confront. It was right there, swirling through his eyes, and in the slightly elevated rise and fall of his chest. In the eyes that left hers for a brief moment to cling to the screen, his fingers spasming a touch before firming again.

Oh, he was affected as much as she was, and she was one hundred per cent sure he'd want to know the sex. But for some reason, he quirked one eyebrow, leaving the decision to her.

To butter her up? To make her feel in control of a situation *he* ultimately controlled?

Genie didn't care. *Couldn't.* Because all this was suddenly too much.

'I prefer to wait. *Gracias,*' she tagged on.

Dr Dominici nodded briskly, then went through a list of caretaking advice. Finally, she hit a button on the screen, then held out two squares of glossy paper, one to each of them.

Genie took it, heart hammering and throat clogging when she looked down at her child. Seve scrutinised his intently, then slid it into his pocket.

Five minutes later, they were back in the hallway and the tension was creeping back.

'I need a moment…' she started, then realised it sounded as if she were asking permission. She cleared her throat. 'I have things to do. I'll come and find you when I need to talk.'

'Genie.'

Again that wave of suppressed emotion was evident in his voice. Her belly clenched, half in alarm and half in anticipation. But layer by layer, the emotions dissipated, leaving his face as smooth as cold glass.

'I'll see you at lunch.'

He walked away without a backward glance.

And she escaped to her bedroom, pacing the living room as she clutched the photo of the child growing in her belly.

When she eventually flopped down onto the sofa and dragged her beloved laptop close, Genie wasn't surprised to find an email from the project manager in Norway. She barely went past the *Due to unforeseen circumstances…* before she closed the email.

Whether Seve Valente had a hand in disrupting her project or not didn't even matter. The traitorous relief flowing through her unlocked the cipher of her decision. She had a handful of hours until her self-imposed deadline ended, but it didn't matter any more either.

Staring down at the ultrasound picture, she took a breath.

And made a decision.

Four months later

Genie would be reluctant to admit it openly, but she loved everything about Cardosia.

Four months and thoughts of Norway had receded so far, she struggled to recall why she'd felt so strongly about going there in the first place. Yes, her ambition to discover new and improved ways for communities to realise a sustainable future burned bright, and the auspices under which she'd arrived in Cardosia still stung a little, but her perspective had shifted somewhat.

For starters, because Seve had never made her feel

like a prisoner. And because once she'd got the full picture of what needed to be done in his country, she'd known that her plans could be shelved for the moment. Cardosia was on the brink of ecological disaster.

Maybe all this had happened because Seve knew her better than she knew herself? Knew she wouldn't try to escape? It was a recurring thought that lately triggered mild panic in her. One in a series of alarming fluttering every time she thought of the man whose baby was growing healthy and strong inside her.

And that was the other thing.

Where was her feminine outrage? And why was she referring to their child as *his baby* now, when she'd been spitting nails on the plane when he'd done the same?

She hated to admit it, but he'd been clever in slowly drawing her into the plans he had for using her algorithm for Cardosia. When he'd shown her the scale of devastation the mining and agricultural plundering was causing, she'd been shocked. Then she'd got to work.

Her algorithm had predicted and devised shortened steps to reclaiming the land, much to the delight of Cardosia's scientists.

Even more impressive was discovering that he'd been secretly buying the desecrated land and handing it over to a nature trust after guaranteeing it would be ecologically maintained. But there were still astonishingly large areas where urgent help was needed.

Finding out during the course of her work that the man responsible for the shocking state of the Cardosian economy was Seve's uncle, Lorenzo Valente, had brought her up short. And when she'd mentioned his name at dinner and received a frosty response from Seve, she'd known to leave the matter alone.

Seve and the team he'd gathered to implement his plans were in a race against time. She was better off concentrating her energies on her contribution to his essential project.

And if she liked it a little bit too much when he praised her for the work her algorithm had achieved, it was a reaction she wisely kept to herself.

What was occupying more and more space in her mind was the trouble she was having analysing why he'd *stopped* asking her to marry him.

For the first month, he'd steadily demanded she give him her decision. Aided and abetted by an eager Lita, who freely expressed that she would love nothing more than for them to wed.

And then he'd stopped. Cold turkey.

Which, of course, had triggered her agitation.

Did he not want to marry her any longer?

The heated eyes that followed her around and the drift of his fingers over her arm, her back of her neck, and, oh, God, her growing belly, said otherwise.

The worst of it was when he travelled to San Martina, the capital city of Cardosia, or even overseas for a few days. It was illogical to torture herself with thoughts of who he was seeing, whether it was of the female persuasion. They owed each other no fidelity after all.

And yet…she missed him with a fervour bordering on insanity.

And when he stalked into her tech studio in search of her on his return and his gaze ran feverishly over her as his chest rose and fell in a deep exhale, her heart leapt, even as she convinced herself it was normal. That there was a rational explanation for it.

They shared a child.

It was one such time that he lingered on his return, sprawling his six-foot-three-inch frame on the long sofa he'd insisted was placed in the basement studio so she could take breaks.

Once he'd conducted that thorough scrutiny that involved running his eyes all over her body, then lingering on her belly, he looked around her work space.

'I have countless rooms in this house and on the estate you can use. Or I can have one built to purpose for you. Why do you choose to hide in the basement?'

She started to shrug but the eyes boring into hers stopped her. Over the past four months, she'd discovered they shared an interest in many facets of their lives. More than she would've thought possible. She'd seen first-hand how much he cared for his country and the environment.

Equally significantly, they were sharing the most important event possibly of their lives.

Certainly of hers.

And while his first barb about her previous basement-dwelling had stung, he'd done it out of ignorance. No one on earth knew what that previous space had meant to her because she'd never shared it.

So enlighten him. So he'll think better of me?

She swallowed the *yes* that rose far too readily to her throat.

Those instances were arriving far too frequently. She'd need to watch that or—

'The longer you take to answer my question, the more intrigued I become.' His languid repose was deceptive. Yet she was drawn to it like prey to a majestic jungle cat. The misleading conviction that she could sidle up and stroke him was all too real and, no matter how much her logical brain tried to warn her that she was straying into dangerous territory, she still couldn't resist the intoxicating danger of baring herself to him. Of basking in that magnificent aura he exuded so effortlessly.

But this feeling—so intense, so raw—was out of her comfort zone. God, everything about Seve Valente had been way out of her sphere of comfort from the moment they met.

A furtive glance at him showed him still relaxed. Intensely alert—because that was his natural state—but giving off an air of recreation that was…soothing. She almost laughed at the description.

Soothing and Seve didn't go hand in hand. Was he making an effort?

Should she?

She frowned inwardly at her own flailing. 'I'm at a loss as to where to start,' she confessed reluctantly.

He nodded. 'That suggests there's a deeper meaning behind your choices?'

She shrugged, still unsure she should be baring herself like this. 'Isn't there always?'

'No. Some nerds just prefer the stereotype,' he said with a trace of amusement, which dissolved as he continued to watch her with hawkish eyes. 'You're not one of them.'

'Probably because I'm not a nerd.'

'No, you're not. You're much more,' he said with the kind of matter-of-factness kings and gods tossed about with conceited abandon.

And, damn him, it had the desired effect. To know that he recognised the special circumstances behind her previous and present actions…mattered. So before she could think further on it, she blurted, 'My parents used me for power and prestige from when I was six to fifteen.'

CHAPTER SEVEN

HE STIFFENED, his posture no longer as relaxed as it'd been seconds ago. He didn't move much, but the intensity in his gaze increased, searing and searching, demanding more.

And Genie had no choice but to give now she'd opened the forbidden box of memories.

'At first it was signing me up for quizzes and maths contests they said would help with bills and to pay for my educational equipment.' She paused, the lump in her throat making it hard for her to swallow.

Superfluous emotion.

She wanted to bat it away but for the first time since Dr Douglas died, Genie found herself readily steeping herself in his counsel. Or was it because it closely echoed Seve's own words the first time they'd been together?

'Let yourself feel. Don't try to rationalise it. Whether it's pain or pleasure, feel it. Both heal.'

Yes. The voice started off as Dr Douglas's and curiously grew deeper, accented, with distinct tones of the man watching her. Waiting for her to bare herself further.

She shook her head free of the muddling sensations.

'It then grew to radio shows and TV appearances and international chess matches.'

A tic rippled through his jaw. 'They were using your genius to line their own pockets.' It wasn't a question but a rapier-sharp statement.

The naked disapproval and quiet rage made more emotions unravel through her. 'Yes. They had no clue how my brain worked or how to have the simplest conversation with me, but they were quick to brag about how much money my intelligence had made them in a particular financial quarter. And because I was a child, they controlled everything. So they could get a big house and employ a full-time minder to look after me while they travelled the world, spending the money they'd made off me.'

'They neglected you,' he confirmed through clenched teeth. 'Completely.'

Again, Genie suspected she was letting herself down by basking in his righteous indignation on her behalf, but in that moment, she didn't care. It felt…*good*. Hadn't Dr Douglas urged her to accept that positive emotion in those rare moments it happened?

'Yes, they did,' she responded, sucking in a breath when something cracked in her chest. Perhaps it was finally speaking it out loud.

'What happened when you were fifteen?' he pressed.

'They died in a boating accident. They were testing out a speedboat they'd leased during a holiday in the south of France when it overturned at high speed. They both drowned.'

A rumbling volcano blazed in his eyes. 'Where were you? Tell me you weren't with them?'

She shook her head, then shivered in recollection of

the fear and abject loneliness she'd felt when the two policemen had delivered the horrible news. 'I was at home, in the basement, writing security code for a Swiss bank they'd made a deal with. I couldn't even stop to go and see my dead parents because they'd locked me into an impossible deadline. I finished it in time to attend their funeral.' She paused, a part of her stunned that she was peeling back so many painful layers. But she was on a course she couldn't abandon, like a string of code she had no choice but to see through to completion. 'But that wasn't the worst of it.'

His eyes swept down for a moment, then rose to pin her. 'What was worse than burying your parents when you were fifteen?'

She couldn't sustain the eye contact; his was too penetrating and Genie suspected hers probably showed far too much raw emotion. She hadn't quite perfected the knack of hiding her feelings like him. Her gaze dropped to the gentle swell of her stomach.

At six and a half months, her stomach was well pronounced. Resting her hand on it, she sucked in a long sustaining breath.

'It's burying your parents when you're fifteen then finding yourself in foster care before the sun sets on the same day.'

He jerked forward, his elbows landing on his knees as he cursed darkly in Cardosian under his breath. 'They didn't provide for you?'

She exhaled shakily. 'No. They didn't bother to put a guardianship in place should anything happen, so I was destined for foster care. I also discovered the house was rented, not owned, and they were in rental arrears. Much like with every other luxury they'd helped themselves to. They'd perfected the art of living excessively beyond their means. In fact, the only thing I owned were the clothes in my wardrobe and my laptop. Even the more expensive tech equipment was on lease agreement.'

'What about the deal with the Swiss bank?'

'They'd already collected on it and the money was gone.'

Eyes filled with banked fury rested on her. '*Dios mio*, Genie...'

She looked away because something in his eyes promised far more danger. The kind that *warmed. Comforted*. Made this sharing almost...*okay*.

This should've been an information-delivering exercise. A means for him to see why she preferred the workspace she preferred. Even if, inherently, the choice was based on emotion?

She shrugged the probing voice away while attempting to push away the warmth burrowing inside her. He evoked far too many of those feelings in her lately, and it was becoming too convenient to blame it on pregnancy hormones. 'Pity isn't useful. I found a way around my situation.'

'It wasn't pity. Trust me, I know what that feels like.'

Her head snapped up and their gazes collided. His shadowed a touch, as if he regretted his revelation. Before she could ask him to elaborate, he asked, 'How did you get around the situation?'

'By shortening my time in foster care to one single month,' she said, striving for the same matter-of-fact tone he'd used earlier, and missing by a mile. Because that month had been the most miserable of her already miserable life thus far, and what had come afterwards had been a mix of terror and loneliness, the residue of which she hadn't ever shaken off, despite Dr Douglas's help.

'One *month*? How? What happened after that?' Seve bit out.

She allowed herself a smile, even though she usually hated gloating, especially over those circumstances. But she'd come through the harrowing ordeal stronger. If not fully in control of her life—because she'd never been quite successful in ridding herself of the abject loneliness—at least with the final say over who she let beneath her guard. 'I ran away from my foster home and started a company that bought the building that eventually served as my head office.'

'How?' he rasped again.

'I'm determined. I'm sure you know that about me. And it's astoundingly easy when you've just written code for a Swiss bank. I hired myself out to companies wanting similar work who didn't bother to ask how old I was. I used the money to acquire shell companies and used *those* to buy a building.'

The slightest widening of his eyes was the giveaway that she'd impressed him. 'And then what?'

'A few keystrokes when you know what you're doing is all it takes. I erased myself from most databases and hid from the system in the basement of the same building I bought. Even then I'd had enough of well-meaning men in suits who claimed to have my best interest at heart but insisted my continued well-being would proceed smoother by letting them help me hone my intellect. I disagreed. So I made myself a home in the basement of my building and I stayed there until I turned eighteen.'

Shock shrouded his face and the hands hanging down between his knees bunched for a few seconds as he said sharply, 'You lived *alone* down there in that square box for three years?'

A peculiar mixture of pride and shame fizzled through her. 'Just about. I was a few weeks from turning sixteen when my parents died. And my choices were limited. I didn't want to be an unwanted burden on anyone or let anyone else dictate my future. Especially the government.'

His nostrils flared and he raked his fingers through his hair. 'Because the two people who should've made your welfare their priority didn't.'

More emotion shook through her. 'Yes.' Her voice quivered with her answer.

He rose from his seat and approached, slowly, prowling languorously as if he didn't want to spook her.

For the longest time, he just stared down at her.

She struggled not to fidget but it was hard when she could almost feel the atomic particles colliding from their proximity. Did every couple who had created a child between them feel this way? This constant edginess as if something seismic was about to happen?

No, she answered her own question. She was certain this was unique to them. Unique and ultimately detrimental if left unguarded against.

And yet she didn't protect herself when he lifted his hand and caught a strand of her hair between his fingers. When he toyed with the silken tresses for an age before transferring that riveting gaze to hers. 'You are a formidable creature, Genie Merchant. But while this is familiar territory and comforting for you, you don't need to hide any more. You have more than earned the right to step out into the light now.' His gaze raked her face intensely before he added, 'And in the light is where you belong.'

The words were low and deep, rumbling through her like a seismic event until it stopped precariously close to her heart. Until it made her so weak, she raised her hand, braced it against his chest as he continued to play with her hair, to stare deep into her eyes, absorbing her every reaction.

Her fingers curled into warm, solid muscle. That weakening intensified.

And before she knew it, she was surging up onto her tiptoes, straining for more of that warmth, that connection, that *feeling* she'd avoided for so long because she'd equated it with weakness, but now craved above all else. For good or ill, she wanted it.

And she would have it.

He met her need, tunnelling his fingers into her hair to cradle her skull, while his other hand braced beneath her body, easily supporting her as his wickedly sensual lips claimed her with unfettered passion.

She was moaning long before his tongue swept past her willing lips to tangle with hers. To stroke with such sensual mastery, she lost her train of thought.

'*Dios mio.* You're intoxicating,' he stated hoarsely when they separated. His fingers drifted down her temple to her cheek, then he traced the outline of her mouth. 'You glow with our child and your joy is enthralling to watch.'

'I was terrified when I found out I was pregnant. It felt...daunting,' she found herself confessing. She'd already bared so much of her secrets, pain and loss. Why not one more?

'But not so much any more?'

She shook her head. 'Not lately, no.'

'Good. You can rest in the assurance that we will always do what is right by our child.'

Something shrivelled inside her at his words. Genie couldn't quite pin it down, but a cool breeze swept over her, dampening her fervour.

It grew colder when, with one last feather-light touch, he stepped back. 'I'll let you finish your work. But from now on, I'll escort you upstairs to lunch every day, and you'll take more breaks to eat and relax. *Entendido?*'

A sliver of that warmth crept back. When was the last time someone cared enough about her like this? *Never.* 'If you insist.'

Dark eyes gleamed with immovable intent. 'I do. Very much.'

And it was as he was leaving that it struck her that she could do something about this feeling. At the very least, she could ensure she wasn't left with these yawning feelings of uncertainty whenever he went away.

Because surely as a wife she would have rights?

Besides the kidnapping their dealings so far had been above board. Deep inside she knew he was a man who held himself to a high standard.

Enough to abstain from sex indefinitely?

Have sex with me if that's the roller coaster you want to jump on.

The thought sent shivers through her, which were doused when thoughts of the end impinged. Dear God. Was she really considering marrying him just so she could ensure he didn't stray into another woman's arms? When she'd explicitly stated that she had no intention of falling into his bed again? What did that make her?

Selfish. Self-centred. Self-absorbed. Human?

That last plaintive question echoed in her own voice, not Dr Douglas's. And when it trailed away, she was no closer to satisfying herself that she was making a sound decision. Which unfortunately threatened her concentration for the rest of the day and in the days that followed.

Days when Seve arrived mid-morning, at lunch and mid-afternoon, as promised, to ensure she took breaks. To walk outside with her, where cool drinks appeared as if by magic at vantage points. And at one spot under a large Cardosian mesquite tree, a picnic had been laid out.

She was enjoying a glass of her now favourite drink—which she'd discovered was a combination of guava, mango and a dash of alcohol-free Cardosian *hierbas* poured over tons of ice—when she felt his gaze on her.

'The doctor is returning tomorrow. Are you still determined not to find out the sex of our child?' His deep voice was laced with amusement.

Dressed in loose linen trousers and a white polo shirt and relaxing with his back against the tree, he was the picture of masculine health and vitality, made even more potent by the impressive bulge between his thighs accentuated by his crossed ankles.

Her face heated when she realised she'd been staring far longer than was polite. Clearing her throat, she attempted to get her brain to track. 'There's nothing to be gained from knowing. It won't make the pregnancy go any faster. My only concern is that he or she is healthy.'

'You know Lita will take it as a personal affront that

your refusal is blocking her from making a list of suitable names, don't you?'

The laughter that burst out of her surprised Genie. Seve too, if the fierce glint and fixed stare were indications. But then his grandmother had become a delightful fixture in her day. She shared at least one meal with the old lady and although she was close-lipped about her grandson's past—because Genie had attempted to garner a few titbits after his reaction to his uncle's name—they got on very well.

So much so that Genie had started to embrace the idea that not all family was all bad. That maybe there was something worth hanging onto regardless of what happened with her and Seve once the baby was born.

'She'll make the list regardless. Just as I'm sure she's secretly designing nursery and christening gowns.' Her statement held a question.

Which Seve blatantly ignored with a shrug. 'I reserve the right not to incriminate myself.'

She continued staring at him as her curiosity mounted. 'Will I have to fight you on names too when the time comes?'

The mood altered a touch, his gaze growing cool when he answered, 'I'm not one of those men who insists on their child taking their name to perpetuate some lofty idea of worthiness or virility.'

She sat up against the half a dozen cushions laid out for her comfort, tugging the light blanket around herself. 'You're named after your father.' She'd discovered as much in her research but not much beyond that. 'It's not a stretch to believe your reasoning stems from this.'

He stiffened and once again Genie suspected she'd strayed onto a red zone. But while she mourned the

loss of their easy conversation and laughter of minutes ago, a newly discovered yearning wanted to keep
transiting through this danger and discomfort. This...
roller coaster.

Dr Douglas would call this progress. And hadn't
Seve himself claimed that roller coasters eventually
ended, leaving abiding feeling?

Her abiding feeling before she'd stepped on the path
was that she wanted to know him more. She'd bared
herself to him against every self-preserving caution.

'If there was ever a blatant example of a man using
his offspring to over-inflate his ego, then I was it for
my father. Hell, both my parents.'

The words were tossed out with icy contempt but
Genie suspected he wasn't even aware of the bitterness
coating his voice. His gaze was trapped in the middle
distance, his languid pose replaced by pure tension.

'Lita doesn't seem like the kind of woman who would
sit by and let you be treated that way.'

His face hardened further, as if this truth was even
more caustic. 'She isn't. Which was why they cut her
out of their lives and by extension mine until I went to
find her when I turned eighteen.'

'They deliberately kept you two apart?'

One corner of his mouth lifted but his expression
was humourless. 'She didn't hesitate to make her feelings known about how her son and daughter-in-law
were mistreating her grandson, only bringing him out
to display him to their guests when it benefitted them to
play the parental role. At some point, she begged them
to let me live with her permanently. They refused of
course. It didn't suit my father to be seen as a neglect-
ful parent, even though he fitted the label. And once

he passed, my mother attempted to pick up where he'd left off. I'd made my first ten million and she felt it was time to leverage her son's accomplishments for social elevation. I hear she still does with her Z-list friends in Buenos Aires.'

Genie gasped. 'Your mother is alive?'

'Very much so. But since the only use she had for me were bragging rights she could gain from having a billionaire son, we parted ways a long time ago.'

Silence reined over their picnic, Genie fighting the strong urge to reach out.

She'd gone with her instincts far too much lately. And these raw emotions were too potent to trust. For all she knew, it was the wrong social cue.

Screw logic. Just feel.

'I don't know if those traits attracted them to one another or whether she was corrupted by my father later, all I know is that family was secondary to him. His primary raison d'être was to elevate himself first and foremost, by whatever means necessary. Fully endorsed by my uncle.'

A jolt went through her at his volunteering this morsel. 'Lorenzo?'

Chilling bleakness entered his eyes. 'I don't know who influenced whom about my upbringing but the worst of it came from him.'

Her mouth dried. 'What did he do?'

Tense moments ticked by when he said nothing, his mouth a thin, forbidding line. When his fingers tightened, she wanted to reach out, to lay her hands over his in reassurance. But she held still, gave him the space he needed.

'He couldn't father children of his own, so I became

his surrogate son with my father's blessing. He was rich and influential enough to sway my parents to his thinking about my upbringing.' His tension ratcheted up until she feared he would snap from the force of it. 'Including administering routine corporal punishment when I was deemed to have misbehaved.'

Genie gasped. 'No.' She didn't realise her hand had shot out to cover his clenched fists until he looked down.

For an eternity they remained still, then his nostrils flared in a loud exhale. 'Oh, yes. They believed being belted on a regular basis would make me a proper man.' The words crackled with bitterness.

Something in her chest cracked as puzzle pieces slotted into place. 'Is that…is that why you didn't want a child of your own?' she ventured softly.

Shadowed eyes rose to meet hers. 'Lita is the only family I trust. But she's not going to be around for ever.' He shrugged. 'The human psyche is a labyrinth. Some things are worth the risk. I didn't think bringing a child into a family plagued by dysfunction and abuse was one of them.'

Her heart lurched. 'Do you still think that?'

His features darkened further. A muscle ticked in his jaw and his gaze lowered to the blanket. 'Like you, I don't accept failure as an option,' he said, his voice driven with purpose. Perhaps even a determination to prove he could succeed where his father and uncle had failed?

It wasn't the resounding *no* she'd hoped for. But then didn't she have her own misgivings about her looming role?

His trauma wasn't on par with what her parents had

done to her, but it resonated, making her wonder if this was what had drawn her to him.

They both carried scars from a past filled with hurt.

The very possibility of such a kinship cracked something tight and hard inside her, a firewall against her loneliness that she realised had been battered and softened in the months she'd been in Cardosia.

Long after the picnic had ended, Genie couldn't harden herself back up again.

On her return to the suite she'd grown ridiculously attached to, she paced. At a much slower clip than before but the vastness of the rooms and the added square footage of the terrace served their purpose.

She'd agreed to stay until the baby was born.

But she was also locked in contractually with Seve's project for the next few years. A project she believed in. Why not take the last step?

They'd both witnessed the deep flaws in their upbringing. Enough to avoid the pitfalls in their own parenting. And as Seve had repeatedly pointed out, weren't they better doing this together than apart?

As if agreeing, Genie felt the softest kick in her womb.

Breath catching, she sank down on the bed and cradled her bump.

'Is that what you want, little one?' It wasn't illogical to talk to her baby. Not when the science had proved it was an effective means of communication. Encouraged even.

So...forget logic. Just feel.

But not too much. Because feelings of bonding love with her baby were one thing.

Letting her firewall be completely eroded and baring herself to emotional desolation from Seve—a man accepting fatherhood because it'd been thrust on him—was another.

CHAPTER EIGHT

SHE MADE SURE to keep as much emotion out of it as possible by lingering after breakfast and sharing another cup of tea with Lita until after Seve left for his study, before following him.

She swallowed the nerves eating at her and barely waited for his prompt to enter after knocking before stalking in, and promptly stumbling to a halt.

Genie was sure he didn't plan it that way—the man she'd come to know didn't chase after vanity—but once again he was bathed in worshipping sunshine, the rays lovingly detailing every perfect sinew and curve, every symphony of movement.

She was frozen in rapt appreciation when he looked up from the documents he was studying, his pursed lips easing when he saw her. But that look reminded her of the formidable powerhouse behind the Valente name. That he had a global empire beyond the borders of Cardosia, one maintained with an iron but very successful fist of his stock value, was an indication.

'Genie, did we forget to discuss something?' he asked, although his tone implied he'd forgotten nothing.

Prodding herself to move, she approached and stopped at a sensible distance where, if she was lucky, she wouldn't have to breathe in his enticing masculine scent on top of everything else. 'We didn't. This is an unscheduled visit to tell you that I've made my decision. I'll marry you.'

She had the pleasure of witnessing Seve caught in wordless shock for a handful of seconds.

Then the usual characteristics flowed. The gleam of triumph in his slate-grey eyes. The imperial nod that suggested he was pleased she was finally seeing things his way.

Then of course that smooth uncoiling of his body from his chair, the well-oiled symmetry of his stride as he ignored her silent plea and brought all that power and sexiness and heavenly scent into her space.

Surrounded her with it.

'This is unexpected excellent news, *pequeña*,' he rasped, his gaze raking her intently as if he hadn't seen her at the breakfast table ten minutes ago.

Feeling all kinds of salacious heat prowling through her, she folded her arms, ignoring the mild discomfort of doing so over her protruding belly.

'My project is on hold for the foreseeable future but I can still work on many more that aren't mine.'

'With mine a priority of course,' he inserted, his eyes still doing that laser-beam thing on her face, absorbing every reaction.

'As per the contract, yes.'

'And those are your only reasons? You don't need to rush off somewhere else to save the world?' Was that an edge in his voice?

She shrugged, even though her heart was beating faster than it had a minute ago. 'Your argument had merit.

I'm not averse to trying to do this together. With the option to dissolve the partnership if it proves fractious.'

His lips compressed. 'How very…clinical. Are you sure there are no other reasons?'

She frowned. 'What other reasons could there be? I'm not intoxicated on high emotion, if that's what you're getting at.'

His eyes darkened, but he nodded a moment later. *Bueno.* The important thing is that you've seen sense. You're doing what's best for our child.'

For the first time, something chafed and snagged inside her. The tiniest hint of resentment that shocked and horrified her. Because it struck her hard that, for a millisecond, she hadn't wanted to be doing this *just* for her child. She'd wanted to be included in the equation that made the whole, not a tossed-aside fraction with no relevance.

'Genie?'

She shook her head, berating herself for the unforgivable flaw. But was it truly a flaw to consider herself a little?

Is there no room for me, *too?*

'Genie.'

The firmer, commanding voice refocused her. Made her aware that he now stood before her, eyes narrowed on her face.

'Yes?'

'What are you thinking?'

She couldn't tell him her thoughts, of course. She hadn't forgotten his cutting words about her basement and how totally absorbed she could be in her work. Mention that she'd been selfishly thinking of how she wanted some attention too, and she'd be proving him right.

She licked her lips, hunting for a feasible answer, acutely aware that with every second his gaze grew more probing.

'I—' She stopped and gasped, the firm kick in her middle snatching her words, saving her from scrambling for an answer. 'Oh!' Her hand flew to her belly, her gaze darting up to meet his suddenly intense one.

Firm hands gripped her upper arms, his eyes racing over her. 'What is it? Is the baby okay?'

Again that abrasion bruised, but, thankfully, the joy of feeling her baby move soothed it. Momentarily.

'No, nothing's wrong. I just felt the baby move.'

His gaze dropped to her stomach, his attention riveted on the pronounced swell. 'Does it hurt?'

For some reason it provoked soft laughter. 'No. Of course not. It's not even uncomfortable. Only a little... unfamiliar.'

His eyes darkened. 'But beautiful, *si*?' he prompted hoarsely.

'Oh, yes. Very much so,' she murmured, her voice equally hushed, as if terrified to break the moment.

The feeble kick came again and, at her gasp, Seve leaned even closer, watching her hand trace the movement with almost awed eyes. 'May I?' he rasped.

Struck by the profound moment despite having felt several flutters in the past, Genie could only nod.

His hand dropped to hover over her stomach, his gaze rapt on her belly. The moment she felt another movement, she took his hand and guided it to the location. For several seconds, they waited, breathless.

Then the third kick came. His intake of breath snapped off halfway and he made a choking sound. *'Dios mio, eso es increíble,'* he rasped under his breath.

'I've been feeling a bit more movement but the text-books say the kicks will get stronger,' she offered, why, she couldn't exactly say. It felt like something she needed to share.

He nodded but his gaze didn't leave her stomach for an age. And of course, because it was Seve Valente, he was rewarded with two more kicks.

When he raised his head, his eyes were molten with overpowering emotion. Emotion she wasn't averse to opening herself up to. To sharing with him because he was directly partnered in this phenomenal event.

The cadence of his caress shifted, the hand moving over her stomach less searching, more…targeted at a different kind of exploration.

'Wh-what are you doing? Is this another social cue I'm unaware of?' Her voice was breathless because they were still wrapped up in feeling their baby kick. Not because…not because other sensations were swirling around them, intensifying with each passing second. Sensations she wanted to dive headlong into, they were so alluringly potent.

'I should hope so. What is happening is that I'm a red-blooded man, *mi dulce*. The sight of the woman who has just agreed to take my name—*my woman*—ripe with my child, turns me on. I'm not going to apologise for it. Especially when you're this breathtaking with it.'

'Seve…'

'*Sí?*' he drawled as his hand moved to her hip, slowly bunching up the flimsy material of her dress in his strong fist and drawing it up her body. 'Tell me you don't like this,' he demanded as he walked her a short distance to the bare wall of his study.

'I…can't.' The unvarnished truth. Because she liked

his hands on her. It was mind-altering. Comparable only to the euphoria of spinning an elusive code into being.

He tilted his head, aligning his face against hers until his stubble teased her skin, his steady exhale brushing her earlobe. 'Tell me you don't want this,' he breathed, starting a delicious shiver that shimmered down her neck all the way to her toes.

'I... I...' She moaned when his fingers whispered over the top edge of her panties. 'I do. I want it.'

With a gruff sound of satisfaction, he dragged the blunt edges of his nails over the skin above her panty line, eliciting a shaken gasp. Her eyes squeezed shut as decadent sensation washed over her.

'Another first for us, *pequeña*. I too have done my research. Pregnant women are extra sensitive. And I've been dying to experience that first-hand.'

Before she could respond, his fingers were delving beneath the soft cotton, seeking her very needy, very wet centre. Finding it, he released a torrent of Cardosian her brain translated as praise and satisfaction and sheer pleasure at her unfettered response.

Genie sagged in his hold, her back braced against the wall and her head falling forward to rest on his shoulder as his fingers boldly explored her. Minutes passed when he teased and tormented with shallow thrusts and feathery touches.

'Seve,' she half moaned, half protested.

'Shh, *mi hermosa flor*, you will be allowed to bloom in due time,' he growled against her ear, then caught her lobe between his teeth. 'For now, let me explore. Let me pleasure you.'

She trembled, her breaths gasping as two fingers

breached her feminine centre, stretching her channel as he finally satisfied her craving.

'Seve!'

'Ah, *querida*. You're just as gloriously tight as I remember. I can't wait to feel you again when you beg me to claim you.'

The *please* trembled on her tongue right then.

Genie didn't know where she found the strength to bite it back. Perhaps she didn't. Perhaps she was rendered mute by the fingers thrusting inside her, finding and stroking that secret bundle of nerves deep inside, at the same time his thumb circled her clitoris and the arm holding her up relocated to her neck, firmly tilting her head up to meet his fiery kiss.

The triple sensation was too much. *Far too much.*

With a muted scream he swallowed as his due, Genie came apart in his arms, succumbing to the transcendent chemistry cascading through her body, transporting her to bliss.

Eyes still shut, she realised a long minute later that the floating sensation was Seve carrying her across the room, spreading her out on his sofa. When she dragged her eyes open, it was to find him poised over her, his ferocious gaze devouring every twitch and shiver.

'You're so beautiful when you come,' he said thickly. Then stunned her by reaching for her sodden panties and dragging them off her body. 'One more, *querida*. I need one more.'

And swift on the heels of one climax, Genie found herself racing towards another when he dropped to his knees and delighted her with his mouth. She was still gasping in release when he disentangled her fingers from his hair and kissed his way up her body.

God, what he did to her was addictive.

Too addictive.

She couldn't fall under this spell, too. 'This can't happen again,' she blurted.

His eyes darkened. 'What?'

'This. Sex. It can't be part of our marriage.' She needed to retain *some* control.

His nostrils flared and she watched him gather his control with something close to amazement. This was why Seve Valente was a veritable bulwark in the venture capitalist world.

'You have my word that I won't touch you until you beg me to. But bear this in mind, *pequeña*. When you do get around to doing so—and don't bother arguing with me, it will happen—there will be no going back. The next time I spread your thighs and claim you, it will mark the beginning of your permanence in my bed.'

He tucked her hair behind her ear, and she caught a whiff of her essence on his fingers as he trailed a hand down her cheek.

Dear God, but that scent alone was enough to make her consider surrendering *now*. To tell him there was no need to wait, that she was ready to jump—or waddle— into his bed right now.

But that would be illogical.

That would be succumbing to the base needs of her body when her mind should be the only consideration tool at play here. Wouldn't it?

As her thoughts whirled, he crooked a smile, that wicked, decadent, I-know-you-better-than-you-know-yourself smile that should've infuriated her but only made her weaker, made her lean into him. Further branding her with his touch.

Those hands continued to mould her flesh with unapologetic bold caresses. As if the magic he'd just wrought on her had given him free access to her.

Hadn't it?

'Battle with yourself if you must, Genie. But don't keep us both waiting for too long.'

'Is…is that a threat?'

His smile deepened, snatching yet another lungful of air from her. 'Not at all, *mi corazón*. But think how… exceptional it would be to take advantage of the next few months until our child is here to indulge.' He leaned closer and whispered in her ear. 'To be a little selfish and take what you want and not feel guilty about it.'

She gasped, her head rearing back so she could stare into his eyes.

He knew. Of course, he did.

The man had near-sorcerer levels of intuition. And when he followed her retreat, brushed his nose with hers then tormented her by hovering his lips over hers without quite making contact, she suspected she was doomed.

'Let me make this easy for you. We will marry next week. On our wedding night, you will come to me. And we will gorge on each other the way a husband and wife are perfectly entitled to.'

Once again she jerked away, another ripple of shock shaking through her frame. '*Next week?* We can't get married in a week!'

His teeth bared in a breathtaking white smile. 'We are two billionaires with every available resource at our fingertips. Even if I hadn't anticipated your acquiescence and put plans in place months ago, it would've been far from impossible.'

'You…what?'

'Don't act so surprised. Your stubbornness in accepting that this was inevitable didn't stop me from doing what needed to be done.' Still reeling from his words, his proximity, her orgasm, and countless other seismic shifts, she could only whimper when he finally brushed his lips over hers, stared down at her mouth for a ferocious few seconds, then resolutely stepped back. 'My grandmother has spent the last three months making your wedding dress. She's been instructing her favourite dressmaker to keep adjusting it once a week.'

'Your grandmother has made my wedding dress?' Yes, she was aware she was rabbiting his words as if her brain cells weren't firing properly. Could anyone blame her?

She'd walked into this room confident of what she intended to happen next. Instead, he'd pulled the rug from beneath her, starting with two mind-bending orgasms, the aftershocks of which she still experienced every minute or so.

'*Sí*. She, like I, lived in hoped that we would marry before the baby arrived. But she also fully accepts that if it isn't to your liking, the final decision is yours.'

No, she *wasn't* melting inside. It was just the prudent coming to terms with her decisions. But as Seve slipped an arm around her waist and led her from his study towards the *salon* where his grandmother spent most of her mornings, she couldn't help but feel her heart swell with…gratitude. With…*love* for the old woman.

And when the old woman took one look at them, quirked an eyebrow at her grandson, then burst into a torrent of Cardosian at his subtle nod complete with clapping and wild smiling, she told herself the tears prickling her eyes were pregnancy hormones.

When Lita patted the seat next to her and picked up the bell to summon the housekeeper, Seve nudged her forward.

'I will leave you to it,' he murmured in her ear, his breath—deliberately, she suspected—wreaking final havoc on her senses.

But she rallied fast before she was completely railroaded. 'Two. I'll marry you in two weeks.' Hopefully by then this insane roller coaster feeling would've stopped long enough to reassure her that she was doing the right thing.

For the longest moment, he stared her down, imposing his will over hers. When he realised she wasn't going to back down, he exhaled and nodded. 'Two weeks.' Then with a hard, firm kiss, he walked away.

And that was how Genie found herself drowning in mountains of gorgeous tulle, silks and priceless pearls.

And a clutch of irrational jealousy.

Would Lita have made this for any woman Seve had intended to marry or…?

She looked up to find the old woman eyeing her with a knowing look. 'You're his choice, child. No one else.'

The words, murmured low and deep in Cardosian, pierced through her jealousy to soothe something inside her.

'Because of his child,' she said, attempting to stave off the swell of emotion rushing at her.

She shrugged. 'I can't change your mind if you want to believe that. You're one with tall walls no one else can break but you. But I also know my grandson. As much as it pains me, he too has walls no convention will

break. But he's breaking down a part of it. For you. I
don't take that lightly.'

Neither should you.

Genie heard the unspoken words but could only
swallow. Because what could she do? She couldn't of-
fend the old woman, who seemed steeped in her belief,
by telling her that she was wrong about her grandson.
That, yes, while convention didn't matter to Seve, this
one where his child was concerned mattered to him.
And that it had nothing to do with her.

*You're the vessel keeping him warm and healthy. For
now, you're important too.*

The reminder echoed with bracing force. One that
made her gasp despite her every effort to mask it. And
when the old woman reached across to clasp Genie's
hand, she attributed the resurgence of tears to more
hormones.

'Enough talk of walls and conventions. Let's talk instead of colour schemes and guest lists, *si*?'

Throat still clogged, Genie nodded. And was introduced to the sheer genius Seve's grandmother could
conjure up with a needle and thread.

More tears threatened when Genie saw that the dress
had started its life with a smaller waistline and had been
let out several times to accommodate her growing pregnancy. With clever stitching, she saw that there was even
more room should she decide to wait.

But she wouldn't be waiting. For good or ill, she'd
made up her mind.

Despite his rough childhood and rigid stance not to
be a father, Seve had committed himself to this. Col-
laborating with him in bringing up their child was the
most logical course of action.

For now.

And if that commitment altered in future? If he re-gretted it?

She ignored the inner voice, and when she looked down to find her fingers lovingly caressing the pearl-studded tulle skirt, she ignored the deep emotion moving through her too.

What was harder to ignore was the indulging and knowing look in Lita's eyes. 'You like it?' she asked, nodding to the dress.

Swallowing, Genie nodded. 'I love it.' At the woman's continued stare, she added, 'And yes, I will wear it for the wedding.'

The housekeeper, maids and Lita broke into excited chatter. A mobile phone was produced and suddenly they were neck-deep in caterers, designers and assistants making lists.

It carried on for days, and before her very eyes, Genie watched the estate transformed into a stunning wedding showpiece.

The path to the jetty that would be welcoming guests was lined with large bunches of assorted flowers that resembled wedding bouquets. Mini chandeliers were hung from strategic branches in the garden and gazebos.

Long benches stood waiting, ready to be decorated. A team of gardeners clipped, pruned and spruced up the garden until it was just that fraction of an inch past perfection. Where the whole thing seemed like an impossibly beautiful vision.

And that was before Seve appeared at her bedroom door two nights before the wedding and imperiously asked to be invited in.

She'd only seen him from a distance during the day,

striding around the grounds with the butler and estate foreman, issuing instructions that were immediately executed.

Genie wasn't sure why it surprised her that a powerful man whose time was literally worth billions was getting involved in his own wedding preparations.

Maybe because she'd thought such things were beneath him? That he'd leave everything to a delighted Lita to take care of? What did it mean that he was taking personal interest?

'The socially acceptable thing is to invite me in, *querida*,' he drawled lazily after several beats, making her bracingly aware that she'd been standing there blocking the door with her body and staring at him with wide-eyed interest.

After a moment's hesitation, she stepped back and nudged the door wider in silent invitation.

He shut the door behind him before turning to her. Heated eyes took in the silk robe she'd changed into after her long soak in the bath, lingered for a spell before dropping to her bare feet, making her toes curl into the deep, soft carpet.

By the time his gaze rose to meet hers again, her body was reacting with alarming predictability, heating in places, dampening in others and hardening in telltale spots that required her to fold her arms across her chest before she gave herself away completely, and she hurried into her living room, perching at the end of one sofa.

'Did you want something?' she asked, then cringed at her breathless tone.

He watched her with knowing eyes, his nostrils flaring in primitive pre-scenting that absurdly made her hotter as he took a seat.

Without answering, he took in the foot spa Sofia had set out for her use. Although she wasn't on her feet most of the day, Genie was tasked enough with sifting through the various interactive social cues and her work on her own code that she barely had time to put her feet up.

The housekeeper's suggestion that she use the luxury spa had been a godsend, although Lita had pursued her lips and muttered about having a perfectly capable grandson who could perform the same duty better.

Genie had pretended not to hear her then, but now, with Seve's attention again on her bare feet, she could barely rip her mind from images of what that would look like.

Just when she imagined her nerves couldn't be stretched any tighter, that her body would betray her completely by thrusting itself into his arms, he reached into his pocket and drew out an oblong velvet box. The kind she knew contained shiny, expensive things because, over the years, several CEOs and wealthy individuals had tried to woo her services by gifting her similar things.

She'd returned every last one. She had no interest in owning baubles. Had never imagined herself in any circumstance where she would be required to don jewellery.

Until now…

Because she was reaching out for it before she could think twice, her fingers caressing the soft velvet.

'This is yours. I would've given it to you tomorrow but Lita has expressly forbidden me from making contact with you from midnight tonight.' There was wry exasperation in his voice but it was lined with affectionate indulgence.

The kind she'd come to yearn for from Lita and shamelessly gorged on during her interactions with Seve's grandmother.

She tapped on the box, prolonging the moment until she opened it. Fighting—futilely, she expected—the surfeit of emotion she would feel once she did.

'You know I can afford whatever is in here, don't you?' she said, because the constant battle between giddiness and danger raged inside her. She couldn't bear to acknowledge that she might be on the losing end.

'Perhaps you can. But the effect wouldn't be quite the same, would it?'

It was a simply stated truth. Bare and unavoidable. 'No. It wouldn't.'

He nodded. 'There's usually intent behind the offering of a gift that makes it have deeper meaning, no?'

She couldn't exactly pinpoint why she blurted out the answer, 'I wouldn't know. The gifts I've received so far have been driven by ego and the need to gain competitive edge.'

'Then be rest assured, this one is not.' A light gleamed in his eyes as he nudged his chin at her, silently commanding her to open the box.

Genie did, fully expecting to see a cascade of gems tossed into an elaborate creation by the latest in vogue master jeweller. Instead, the single, albeit sizeable teardrop diamond, bearing the proud hallmarks of Cardosian purple, was nestled in a deep yellow gold that spoke of its age. The chain was delicate but strong, the kind you saw in period portraits. Matching earrings glinted on either side of the necklace.

She gasped at the simple beauty of it, her fingers drifting over the chain before brushing the dazzling diamonds. 'It's...beautiful.'

'It belonged to Lita. She wore it on her wedding day. You will wear this on our wedding day. It will please her,' he said, then, after another of those volcanic glances, he rumbled, 'And me.'

Perhaps she was mastering this social cue thing because those last words tipped her into pleasure. Into exhaling shakily before giving a simple, acquiescent nod. 'I will.' Then, with a smile because this was getting easier, she added, 'Thank you.'

Now his gaze was riveted to her mouth, making it tingle and quiver. Making her whole body yearn unbearably.

Her baby kicked as if egging her into doing *something* to alleviate this ache. Was she bold enough? Foolish enough? She'd drawn a line in the sand in his study two weeks ago. Crossing it so soon would be ludicrous. Wouldn't it?

'Have you used that yet?'

She startled a little at the gruff question, and glanced at Seve to find his attention on the foot spa.

'No, I was just about to,' she replied.

He plucked the bottle containing the oil she normally infused the water with and examined it. Then he did something that yet again made the breath leave her lungs.

Seve Valente sat back on the sofa and patted his strong, muscled thighs. 'Allow me?'

And because every muscle in her body attempted to

strain towards him in total compliance, she folded her arms again and raised an eyebrow. 'You're an expert on foot massages?'

'Why don't I let you be the judge?'

She was aware her eyes had grown comically wide. That her pulse was racing much faster than it had moments ago. The baby kicked again. She dropped a hand, laid it on the swell of her stomach, but there was no calming her boisterous baby.

'I see I have an ally,' he said with supreme smugness, his eyes lingering on her belly.

Then, without waiting for a response, Seve rose, picked up the spa and walked out of the room with it towards her bathroom.

The thought that he meant to conduct the massage himself settled in deep, making that tingling a full-bodied event that had no logic whatsoever. But, goodness, it was…addictively good.

By the time he returned to the sofa, sat down and patted his thighs once more, Genie had stopped battling with herself.

Intensely aware of her breathlessness, she angled her body and raised her legs.

Strong fingers curled around her ankle to settle her lower limbs on his legs. The scent of geranium and marjoram drifted through the air as he poured a measure into his hands, warmed it up in his large palms. Then glided them over the top of her foot.

Genie caught her lip between her teeth, barely containing the moan before it slipped free. From the first, his touch had aroused and excited her. Despite this being a stress-relieving kindness on his part, this time was no different for her.

More, it quickly turned into an erotic adventure she hadn't had a single inkling about until the sight of his oiled hands on her feet threatened to induce hyperventilation.

She blushed when the next moan slipped free.

Eyes like molten mercury met hers, the slight parting of his lips making her wish they were devouring her. Dear heaven, what was wrong with her?

Her brain was tired of answering the question so all she heard was the rushing of blood through her ears, and all she could do was grip the edges of her robe with one hand, and surreptitiously bite down on her fist as his expert fingers dissolved the tightness in her with acupuncture accuracy.

It was so good that when her spine melted, she didn't protest. When her nipples tightened, she didn't bother to hide them. It was no use.

Seve knew his effect on her.

'You look like a very fertile enchantress,' he observed thickly. 'A lesser man would be begging for you to cast a spell on him.'

A shade of disappointment threatened to douse the pleasure zinging through her body. 'You're not one of those, of course?'

His barely there smile looked strained around the edges. 'We agreed that any begging between us would be done by you, *querida*. Not me.'

'And you're set on not straying from that course, *señor*?'

He glanced down at her feet, a pinched look invading his features as he stroked his thumb between her first and second toes.

A rough sound left his throat as he followed the movement and shifted in his seat.

It was then that she got a better idea of what was happening to him too. The hard bulge in between his legs against the arch of her foot. The breath hissing between his teeth. The heavy rise and fall of his chest.

With clear reluctance, he caressed her arches one more time, then rose from the sofa. Watching him wipe off his hands, she prepared herself for his departure, but he only dragged fingers through his hair before striding to the other side of the room.

'Should I ask if something is wrong or wait for you to volunteer it?'

'There's something else you need to know. My uncle is attending the wedding.'

The uncle who'd made his childhood hell and was intent on damaging Cardosia just as badly? Genie stiffened. 'Why? You owe him nothing. Am I missing something? I can tell you're not particularly thrilled about it.'

'I'm not,' he bit out, his jaw clenched. 'And I didn't invite him. Lita did. I can't uninvite him without causing unnecessary drama.'

Genie frowned. 'But she knows what he did to you. Why would she?'

His gaze met hers with solemn contemplation, long enough for her to squirm.

'Is it a social cue I'm missing? A rule that says you have to endure someone you dislike?'

Something hard chased across his face. 'It's not that simple.'

'Isn't it? You don't like him, so don't invite him.'

'Sometimes circumstances demand we put our emotions aside.'

As he'd done with her? Was there a logical conclusion she was missing? Something deeper?

'Are…are you trying to prove something to yourself, Seve?' she asked.

He stiffened. 'What if I am?'

Her heart lurched then ached for him.

He'd listened to her past without judgement. Told her it was time to step into the light because she deserved it. Wasn't it time he did the same too? If that meant confronting his uncle, then wasn't she selfish to protest? If this thing they were doing was ultimately to succeed, mutual support was imperative.

She nodded. 'Then let him come. If only to witness first-hand his failure to subjugate you.'

A jolt went through him, as if her words had shocked him. When he started to frown, she rushed on. 'Besides, with the number of guests attending, spending minimal time with him shouldn't be hard at all.'

His mouth quirked without humour. 'Your faith in me is touching, *pequeña*. Unfortunately, he isn't a man who likes to be ignored.'

'If you're telling me to act a certain way around him, I can't guarantee I will.'

For the first time in the last few tense minutes, his lips quirked in a genuine smile. 'I would prefer you to be exactly who you are.'

Genie's spine melted again and she realised she'd started to tense up again. Resisting the absurd urge to smile back, she nodded. 'I will. Thank you.'

Seve watched her for a few more charged minutes. Then he inclined his head. 'Sleep well, *mi dulce*. I will see you at the altar,' he said.

She nodded, her emotions too overwhelming to form words.

With sure strides he went to the door. Opened it. Then looked over his shoulder. 'A lot can happen in thirty-six hours. Ensure that you not turning up isn't one of them.'

Far from being annoyed by his high-handedness, she caught the barest hint of vulnerability in that statement. It was what kept her buoyed that night, and the next.

Right up to the moment Lita kissed her gently on her cheek on the morning of her wedding; told her to take a moment if she needed it.

Right up to the moment she stepped out onto the terrace, dressed in her wedding gown, ready to marry the father of her child.

And the tendrils of uncertainty set in.

CHAPTER NINE

'No NEED TO start a war yet, friend. She's only nine minutes late. I'm told an hour, even two, is standard operating procedure for a bride's tardiness. Of course, that's a theory I never intend to test.'

Seve shot a glare at the man he'd chosen as his best man. The man who was gently teasing him because of that one flicker of his gaze to the terrace doors. Fine, perhaps it'd been more than one.

He could count the number of his true friends on the fingers of one hand.

Alessio Montaldi was one of them.

Although their paths crossed in person only a handful of times in any given year, the flint-eyed Sicilian had an outlook on life that Seve found…agreeable. He possessed a familiar single-mindedness, and by all whispered accounts he'd pulled himself up from dire circumstances as a child to become a formidable businessman.

But what impressed Seve most was that Montaldi held his past close to his chest, just as Seve did. Somehow they'd formed a friendship from behind their individual impenetrable walls.

He'd arrived on his superyacht mid-afternoon yes-

terday and insisted Seve spend his last evening of freedom onboard the vessel. He'd refused, of course. For
some reason spending the night under a different roof
from Genie felt…undesirable.

'You have time to mock when you've also been
checking your phone every five minutes? Tell me it's
not a woman behind that frantic checking.'

'Frantic? Hardly. And no, it's not a woman. Well, at
least not the type of female that attracts my attention.'

'I could pretend I care, or I can—' He stopped, his
breath leaving his lungs when he saw movement on
the terrace. But it was a member of the catering staff.

His jaw gritted as Alessio laughed under his breath
and Lita shot a worried look over her shoulder.

Eleven minutes.

He'd make it a clean dozen before he…what? Did
the unconscionable thing and hunted down his pregnant fiancée and forced her to the altar? In full view
of a watchful Lorenzo, whose presence speared jagged
knives of fury and bitterness through him? Perhaps he
should've listened to Genie and uninvited him. Was
he misguided to pick this occasion to look the devil in
the eye and show him he was…what? Better than him?
That he intended to succeed where his father and Lorenzo had failed?

Yes.

He ignored the tinge of guilt that came with it. Didn't
want to examine if his vigour in persuading Genie to
remain in Cardosia had partly been because he'd needed
to prove to himself that he was…impervious to letting
past trauma and Lorenzo's shadow damage his future.

He shifted as the guilt intensified, but, alongside

it, determination to see this through burned steadily in his chest.

Lorenzo didn't matter any longer save as an obstacle to be disposed of for the betterment of Cardosia. Nothing more.

His presence here was a good opportunity to show him his 'failure to subjugate'.

Genie's words intensified the flame. Re-grounding him.

Dios, where was she? She hadn't changed her mind She'd given him her word.

Hadn't she?

As he thought back over their conversation two nights ago, a stone lodged in his chest. She hadn't actually given the promise. Considering he was marrying a renowned genius, had he allowed himself to be tricked? Perhaps the courtesy of two weeks had been a mistake on his part, considering he'd bided his time for over *four months*.

He should've swept her into his arms and found the nearest church the moment she'd stormed into his office and announced she would marr—

Another movement stopped his chaotic thoughts, and every muscle froze in his body.

'She's here. Maybe it's time to throttle back the murderous intent on your face?' Alessio quipped under his breath, but Seve barely heard him.

He was far too riveted by the sight drifting down the lawn towards him. He wanted to say Lita had outdone herself with the dress, but it was the woman wearing it who created the breathtaking vision. The low scoop of her gown and cinch of the high waistline highlighted her very pregnant state, and Seve was certain he'd never seen her more magnificent.

She carried no flowers in her hand but a circlet of white and purple flowers rested on her crown, her hair elaborately braided and pinned away to leave her swan-like neck on display. Her face bore minimal make-up, and her skin *glowed* underneath the Cardosian sun. And—

Barefoot. She was *barefoot*.

A dismissing of norms or because Genie Merchant, soon to be Valente, was confident enough in her power to simply do as she pleased?

Who cared? She was here.

He took a breath. Then another. But the clamour didn't ease inside him. It'd been building for weeks and, for the first time in his life, he couldn't exactly pinpoint the source of it. All he knew was that he...*yearned*. And while he pondered fatherhood often enough, the total-ity of that yearning wasn't centred around his unborn child but rather the woman carrying it. The rage and kinship he'd felt that day when she'd confessed why she clung to her basement workspace. His shock and elation when she'd blatantly confessed what he made her feel.

He'd wanted *more* of that, he realised.

Had he deluded himself into believing he was mar-rying for one reason when the reasons were manifold?

The soft green grass only accentuated her bare feet, expanding her allure until it consumed him whole. Until he knew, deep in his bones, a fundamental shift had occurred. That he did not want just a connection with this woman through their unborn child or their shared dysfunctional upbringing. He wanted...*more*.

And he didn't have a clue how to get it.

'Seriously, you're beginning to terrify *me*, and I'm the one who triggers terror in others,' Alessio rumbled quietly beside him.

Genie's gaze was momentarily on Lita, who was blowing her a soft kiss. Seve throttled back his rioting feelings, arranged his stance into a less…feral pose, channelling his thoughts into less of his marauding forebears who took without reserve and more of the modern man the world believed him to be.

A deep breath. Less concrete shoulders…

'Much better. Now I suggest you put a ring on it before you show her your true colours.'

His true colours.

His gaze shifted past Genie back to Lorenzo, the man who'd imprinted his merciless scars on him. Were those his true colours? Or could he find it within himself to eject any traces of trauma from his soul?

The older man, who bore an uncanny resemblance to Seve's father, watched him with chilling warning, as if he knew Seve's thought. One eyebrow rose, asking a question Seve had no intention of answering.

Not now.

Not when Genie was three feet away, her eyes set unwavering upon his.

His fearless genius.

'I'm here. Now what?' she asked softly in that defiant way he now knew covered a multitude of vulnerabilities. Vulnerabilities he would ensure were eliminated soon enough.

Beside him, Alessio snorted under his breath.

Seve ignored him and held out his hand to her.

She took it and stepped up beside him. And despite the tremble in her hand and the nerves that made her cast furtive glances his way, Genie Merchant made her vows.

He followed suit, the shifting in him intensifying.

Resetting his life in ways he couldn't quite fathom yet. But he allowed it to happen because, as terrifying as it was, it felt…right.

She was married.

Genie nursed an apple spritzer in place of the over-flowing vintage champagne and tried not to stare too hard at the glittering Cardosian diamond on her finger. Its setting was far more modern and sophisticated than the necklace and earring set Seve had gifted her, but it was no less magnificent.

All around her people laughed and chatted, occasionally casting furtive glances her way.

She supposed it was normal, people taking an interest in the new bride. Or maybe it wasn't, and they just wanted to gape at the obviously pregnant woman Seve Valente had saddled himself with.

The one who'd attended her own wedding without shoes.

She told herself she didn't care. But years of isolation had a way of sinking their claws into one's psyche and it wasn't easy to shake off. So she'd dug deep to find socially acceptable responses to the guests' well-wishing. And once that had dried up, she'd chosen silence.

Seve was talking to his best man, Alessio Montaldi, the man whose intensity rivalled that of her husband, and who tugged out his phone with alarming frequency to scowl at the screen, as if he was willing whatever he was waiting for to materialise. So far without success.

A strong arm curled around her thick waist, and she startled.

Seve.

She thought he'd forgotten about her.

'You're either completely enamoured of your wedding ring or you absolutely hate it. Which is it?' he murmured in her ear, and, curiously, something eased inside her. Because just like with his parting statement two nights ago, there was a touch of uncertainty in his voice that awakened the feeling again.

The feeling that he *cared*. That she *mattered*.

'It's certainly…unique,' she hedged, even now afraid to embrace it. Even though her strong emotions warned her that it might be too late.

That this was a culmination of weeks of her foundation being chipped away by Lita's acceptance, Sofia's soft words, Cardosia's beauty. But most of all, by this man…*her husband*…who evoked feelings inside her no one person on this planet could.

As much as the illogical term confounded her, she was…falling in love with Seve. Probably already had.

'That doesn't quite give me the answer I require,' he pressed, his voice deep, insistent.

She looked up into his eyes and everyone in the room ceased to exist. 'What would you like me to say?' Her voice wasn't as steady as she would've liked, what with that seismic shift creating impossible waves inside her.

'Tell me how it makes you feel,' he said, the words packing more of a punch than she'd expected.

'Why?'

He faced her with his broad back to the room, blocking everyone else out. 'Because I find I like knowing how you feel, Genie Valente.'

'Genie Valente-Merchant. I haven't made up my mind if I want to give up my name yet.'

His nostrils flared but along with it came a whisper of amusement darting across his face. The small crack in his facade again caused emotion to swell. Enough to soften that vulnerable place around her heart.

Enough to make her glance down at her hand and murmur, 'I love the ring, Seve. Very much.'

'And?' he demanded tightly.

For a fraught few seconds, she didn't know what he meant. Then she saw it emblazoned, wild and demanding in his eyes.

I won't touch you until you beg me to...next time...it will mark the beginning of your permanence in my bed.

But would it be demeaning if it was what she...what they *both* wanted? They were married now. She had a right to her husband's body just as much as he had a right to hers. If emotions had crept into the picture, surely it wouldn't alter the fundamental reason for marrying?

The tiny void in her heart said different. Genie ignored it. For now. Instead she opened her mouth to answer. To offer what they both wanted.

But the words locked in her throat when Seve stiffened. She followed his gaze and met the slightly darker grey version of Seve's eyes in the older man who'd kept his distance but watched them since his arrival.

Lorenzo Valente was suave and polished, his suit bespoke and sharp. But it was all a carefully cultivated veneer, like his neatly slicked back hair.

He would never attain the sheer *presence* his nephew possessed. Seve didn't need to announce himself when he entered a room. Lorenzo might inhabit a space, but no one felt his existence until he was right in front of you. Which was probably a dangerous thing.

Judging from the cold lifelessness of his gaze and his reptilian smile when he reached them, she'd do well to remember that.

'I haven't had the chance to personally welcome your bride yet, nephew.' His gaze lingered on her face, then deliberately dropped to her belly. 'Or to congratulate her on the happy addition to our family.'

'Your wishes are noted. But as to my wife and child being part of your family, that'll never happen. You had your chance and you failed at it. Also, your gift will be returned. My wife adores Cardosian diamonds. The tennis bracelet you sent, while beautiful, has questionable sources we'd rather not accept.'

Genie stiffened, then melted against him as her heart swelled. How well he knew her. She hadn't even seen the gift yet but she would've done exactly as Seve was doing.

Even as Lorenzo's face hardened. 'You'd do well to show some respect. And while you're at it, to not poke your nose into matters that aren't your business. I'd hate to have to engage in unnecessary public squabbling with my own flesh and blood.'

'Cardosian business is my business. And respect is earned. Enlighten me in what ways you've earned mine, Uncle?'

Lorenzo gave a humourless smile that chilled Genie. 'You've been overseas too long. Clearly you've forgotten how to respect your elders.'

Seve turned into a pillar of stone. 'Trust me, I've forgotten nothing. Perhaps it's you who should bear that in mind.' His arm circled her waist once more and, despite the warmth of his proximity, a shiver raced through Genie. 'Things have changed and *will* continue to change. How you deal with it is your problem. Enjoy the rest of the reception, Uncle.'

As he steered her away, Genie couldn't shake the inkling that she'd just been used to make a specific point. But just what the point was, she couldn't determine.

Before she could question him, Lita was making a beeline for her.

'Time for a little rest before the evening's events, child.' She cast her grandson a quizzical smile and Genie saw Seve shake his head from the corner of her eye.

Again, she wanted to demand to know what was going on. But he was brushing a kiss on her temple, a second and third on her cheek and corner of her mouth, effectively scrambling her brain.

'See you shortly, *pequeña*,' he murmured, but the edge remained in his voice, the tension in his body.

By the time she'd regained the power of speech, he was halfway across the room, his gaze narrowed on his friend. Again, a silent conversation took place and Genie watched the two men stride towards his study, the tingling at her nape intensifying.

'Come, *muchacha*. Let's get you upstairs.'

She let Lita and her retinue lead her out of the room and by the time she reached her bedroom, Genie was grateful for the breather. Her back ached, the size of her stomach seeming to have grown since she woke up that morning.

Her baby, wanting to make its presence felt, kicked, distracting her from her thoughts. But they soon came crowding back. And since she was installed on her sofa with Sofia gently lowering her aching feet into the spa, Genie cradled her cup of tea, glanced at Lita and went for it.

'What's going on between Seve and his uncle?' she asked. Now wasn't the time to edge her way into the subject.

For a second, the older woman stiffened, but then she gave a smile tinged with sadness. 'A past I'd hoped could be put behind us once and for all. Lorenzo and Seve's father were as thick as thieves, unfortunately not in a way that would make any mother proud. It would be easy to blame Lorenzo for leading my other son astray, but a man creates his own path.' Her eyes speared Genie's and held with that core of steel Lita displayed when she made a point. 'Trust that your husband will not forget who he is,' she added cryptically.

'What do you—?' The question was cut off when Lita, deciding the conversation was at an end, strode away, bustling the other women into their designated roles for the evening party. Genie pursed her lips, attempting to stem the rising disquiet within her.

It didn't work as efficiently as she wished, and by the time she'd changed into the deep champagne-coloured gown with thin gold stripes that made each step she took shimmer, the disquiet had only grown. Low gold pumps were manageable after her foot spa and after a quick refresh of her lip gloss, she was ready.

The first thing she saw when she rejoined the party was that Seve had changed too. His morning suit was swapped for a more casual but bespoke one that matched hers. Hard on the heels of that, she noticed that his demeanour hadn't changed. If anything, his face held that same determination from the day he'd walked into her office demanding she sell him her algorithm.

Her algorithm…

Was that what his uncle had been referring to? No doubt the older man would be aware of what Seve was doing by now.

Unease building inside her, he'd barely reached her when she blurted, 'What's going on? What did your uncle mean earlier?'

Something dark and forbidding flashed in his eyes but a moment later, he'd blinked it away. 'It's nothing for you to worry about, *querida*.'

'I'd be reassured if you enlightened me so I don't make assumptions.'

Again something flashed in his eyes and this time it stayed. Something that surprisingly resembled bleakness. 'You don't trust me, Genie?'

That brought her up short. Not once in her life had trust been demanded of her. Her parents hadn't wanted or needed her trust. They'd simply desired a cash cow they could milk. The authorities she'd had the misfortune of dealing with had merely required her compliance so they could take advantage of her.

But these last few months, she'd lowered her guard and let others in.

Because of Seve.

The rush came again, drowning out an echo of the disquiet. 'Yes, I do.'

The light now burned a different shade, almost consuming her as it stayed on her face. Then he held out his hand. 'Then believe that everything will happen as it's supposed to.'

Genie swallowed the next dozen questions. She

might not be built to simply accept a cipher and patiently wait for it to unravel itself, but, with Seve, she was learning that she could bend whichever way he wanted her to without losing herself. It was a tightrope she was learning to navigate.

Her questions could wait. It was her wedding day.

And while her baby bump stopped her from exerting herself too much, she could sit at the banquet table set out in the garden and watch the sun go down while guests she didn't know laughed and danced. While Lita affectionately pushed tiny dishes Genie's way in a bid to fatten her up, and Seve helped her up when she needed to stretch her legs and rubbed her lower back just when she needed it.

She breathed a sigh of relief when Lorenzo abruptly left but Genie couldn't totally relax because Alessio strode up a minute later.

'It's time for me to say goodbye too.' He reached for Genie's hand and, ignoring the rumble of warning from Seve, pressed a kiss to her knuckles. 'Until we meet again, *dulce*.'

'Did what you were looking for arrive?' Genie asked, indicating the phone clutched in his hand.

Alessio's face morphed, a mixture of harshness and intrigue glinting in his eyes. 'Not quite. But cast your net wide enough and all manner of interesting things get caught in it,' he replied cryptically.

He held out his hand to Seve. And like with many of the people her husband was close to, a secret conversation passed between the two men that set Genie's hackles on alert all over again.

'I will keep you apprised, friend,' Alessio said in rapid Sicilian.

To which Seve replied, 'I am in your debt.'

With a nod, the other man strode away.

CHAPTER TEN

'SHOULD I BOTHER asking why you're indebted to your best man or does this conveniently fall under the trust umbrella too?'

For an age, Seve simply stared at her, then he calmly held out his hand. 'Dance with your husband and tell me which other languages you speak beside Sicilian and Cardosian so I can be on guard. I also find that I'm in dire need to pick up on another conversation.'

'You are avoiding the subject.'

'I'm rescheduling it for when the time is more appropriate.'

His hand remained between them, and, like a puppet on a string, hers rose to slide into his grip. 'Is it accepted to say that being cryptic can be sexy to other women but it just makes me want to grind my teeth?'

A flash of teeth delivered a dazzling smile that didn't quite reach his eyes. 'We've established that you can say whatever you wish to me, *dulce esposa*. But I don't quite believe you about the singular reaction. You can find me sexy and grind your teeth at the same time. In fact, I bet that's what's happening right now.'

He wasn't wrong. The slide of his hand in hers was making her breathing jump and skitter in her chest.

And as they reached the dance floor, something else occurred to her. She stared down at her feet. Well, she tried to but her belly was in the way. 'I'm not very good at dancing. Nor am I sure how we're going to do this with my—'

'Hush, *pequeña*,' he rumbled in her ear. 'Leave the logistics to me.'

Whether by design or coincidence, the sultry beat of a Cardosian samba tune thrummed through the air. In the waning daylight, light and shadows whirled around them, fireflies awakening to join the festivities as Seve took both her hands and moved in loose-hipped, mesmeric rhythm. The first few steps were easy enough to follow and they were soon in sync.

The soft whisper of her gown, the warm breeze, the heated intensity of Seve's eyes and the hands gripping hers…the trust…all interlocked into a divine expression of everything she was feeling inside.

The…love she'd craved for so long and despaired she'd ever find.

The astonishing realisation that the harsh binds of loneliness that had lashed her had unshackled and fallen away without her taking note of it.

That should she choose to, she could wake up every morning and be a part of a true family. With her baby. Because, surely, that was what Seve had meant when he'd demanded permanence?

Was it truly within her grasp?

It felt too powerful, too awe-inspiring to fully accept. Like the heart-stopping moment before the final string of code fell into place and you realised something phenomenal was about to occur.

Could she—?

Her thought froze when Seve slid a finger beneath her chin and raised her gaze to his. '*Mi preciosa*, what troubles you?'

She realised her eyes were prickling with the power of her emotions. 'It seems I'm back on the roller coaster again.'

His nostrils flared. 'Experiencing it in a good way?'

She nodded. 'In a great way. I… I…'

Love you.

She wasn't sure why the two words collapsed and died on the tip of her tongue. Perhaps it was a social cue thing. Neither of them was overly flamboyant. So perhaps this was a pointer that she needed to say it in private.

Later?

The twang in her chest suggested otherwise.

But Seve was lowering his head, brushing his lips lightly over hers, twirling her around and nudging her close, so her back was to his front. And her breath was stuttering all over again because he was raising her arm to twine it around his neck, trapping it there with one hand, while his other sneaked around her waist to cradle her belly.

'Oh…'

His hips nudged hers, guiding them into a sensual sway. 'That's it, *mi esposa*. Sink into it. Let it wash over you.'

He held her like that through three songs, until her back protested and the baby's kicks grew too distracting. Then Seve swung her into his arms and gave a very brief speech to their guests before striding with her towards the far end of the lawn.

Where a helicopter waited.

'We're leaving?'

'For the next several nights, yes.'

'I can't help but think you're kidnapping me again.'

'Technically, I haven't freed you from captivity yet,' he said dryly, the teasing glint in his eyes setting her alight.

Her lips curled in a smile, and as she stared up at him the last of her resistance melted away.

She was in love with Seve Valente.

What better way to celebrate her wedding night than in his arms? In his bed. Where she could confess…as much as her limited knowledge of these things would allow…what she felt for him.

He caught her smile and something shifted in his eyes. A question? An acknowledgement? A flash of primal acceptance of his due?

Whatever it was, it thrilled and left her breathless, making her cling to him all through the twenty-minute ride into the mountains.

To the sprawling cabin set in the middle of dense woods that made it all the more perfect. From above she saw soft gold light scattered throughout the sprawling structure.

The air was cooler up here. When they alighted from the chopper, Seve shrugged out of his jacket and draped it over her shoulders, infusing her with his warmth and scent.

Hand in hand, they walked up the stone path that led to solid oak doors.

The moment the doors shut behind them, she heard the rotors of the chopper again. 'Are we on our own?' she asked.

He nodded, guiding her further into the vast living

room, which had oak beams, sumptuous coats and a gentle fire roaring in the hearth.

Seve's hands drifted down her middle and traced over the swell of her stomach before he responded. 'Sí. If you're worried about being away from civilisation, the pilot isn't going very far, and the butler, doctor and a few staff are minutes away.'

She hadn't fully taken in that there was a niggle until he volunteered the information. Then her shoulders relaxed. Kicking off her shoes, she turned and slid her arms around his neck, an act that was getting alarmingly easy and addictive. The circle of Seve's arms was beginning to feel like…belonging.

Like home.

'I'm not worried,' she replied, then realised it was true. She'd admitted her trust and she knew Seve would do anything to protect their baby.

His lips curved against her neck and his hands moved from her belly to her hips, kneading firm circles into her flesh that made her moan. 'Good. It's been a long day. I should let you rest,' he said, but she caught the thick need in his voice.

The same need echoing through her.

'Yes, you should,' she said, her attempt to tease sending a shiver through her own body. But he responded, his breathing a little erratic as he pressed a kiss to the sensitive skin beneath her ear. 'But I'm guessing you'd rather keep me up for a little longer?'

'Sí, mucho,' he growled, his hands digging deeper.

Genie was fairly sure he wasn't aware how firmly he held onto her. She didn't call his attention to it because she liked it. Liked him being so intensely enthralled. Liked being needed this much.

It was so new that she was still discovering the unique facets of it with far too much enthusiasm. So she turned, presented her back to him, and swept her hair to one side. 'Help me with my zip?'

His nostrils flared and her skin tingled where his eyes feasted on her. Confident fingers drew down the long zip until it bared her back, and she cupped the dress to her chest to keep it from slipping to the floor.

When she glanced at him, the look in his eyes was ferocious. Earthy and primal. Devouring every inch of flesh he could find. 'Cease the torture, *mi esposa*. Say the words.'

'I want you, Seve. I need you to take me.'

His chest expanded on a heaving breath that stayed locked, making him almost appear a beast. *Her beast*. 'And? Tell me you know what that means.'

Emotion shook through her, solidifying her decision. This wasn't a frivolous one-night stand. This was a commitment. For life. 'I do. I come to your bed, I stay in your bed.'

The breath expelled from his lungs as he prowled around to face her, his chiselled features tightening as his fevered gaze roved all over her, stamping his complete ownership of her.

Firm hands grasped her arms, lifted them away so her gown pooled into a silky froth at her feet, leaving her in only her white lace panties.

For an eternity, he stared at her ripe body, his throat moving convulsively as he swallowed. '*Dios mio.* You're a goddess. *Mi diosa perfecta.*'

'Hardly,' she tried to counter, but her hitched voice betrayed her thrill at his words.

'Oh, yes. Your belly is swollen with my child and it's the most perfect sight I've ever seen.'

Genie couldn't help it. Tears filled her eyes, words of love tripping to her tongue.

He made a rough sound. His hands cupped her face, brushing away the tears before they fell. Then he swooped, sealing her mouth with his before she could speak the words. And then she was lost in sensation, clinging to him even as he shed his clothes, a mixture of frustrated laughter only building the blaze of lust and connection between them.

When he fetched fat cushions and laid her down on the thick rug before the fire and proceeded to kiss every inch of her body, Genie buried her fingers in his hair, closed her eyes and lost herself to pure sensation and magic created by his hands and lips and tongue.

She was delirious by the time he propped her up on her hands and knees, her senses on fire. Genie moaned when his hands glided down her spine, thick words of praise falling from his lips.

'I need you,' she whimpered at the feel of his touch caressing boldly between her thighs, stoking her wet centre.

'Aren't you forgetting one last thing?' Seve rasped, his body hard, warm and primed for her.

Her brain lagged for a few seconds before she gasped. 'You're not really going to make me beg?'

'A deal is a deal, *pequeña*,' he stated hoarsely, his tongue gliding out to lick his lower lip as anticipation carved his features into perfect stone.

'Please, Seve. Please take me,' she obliged breathlessly, too far gone to equivocate. Then took pleasure in watching him shut his eyes on a groan as he grappled for control.

Then he was surging into her, the skill and intensity of him making her cry out in sheer bliss. Perhaps it was the weeks upon weeks of roller-coaster emotions she'd been through that had brought her up to this point, or it could've been the sheer bliss of taking him into her body without protection, but Genie felt the power of the moment. More tears flowed and she didn't bother to stem them.

Her life was no longer a desolate landscape. She had a husband and a baby.

What more could she ask for?

Just one final thing.

Seve accepted what needed to be done as he curled his body around Genie's, his heart still racing from the transformative sex they'd just had.

He'd stalled for long enough.

They'd been in his mountain cabin for seven days. One glorious, uninterrupted week he'd been uncertain he'd settle into—because he rarely took vacations—but had quietly relished nonetheless. Days when, every time he caught a glimpse of Genie's belly or the flash of the Cardosian diamond on her finger, or, hell, even saw her bare feet, it produced a wild kick in his chest he repeatedly had to clench his gut to absorb.

And Genie…

He enjoyed indulging her. She made him feel… *lighter*. And he would feel lighter still once he exorcised Lorenzo from his life once and for all.

Genie's intelligence had gifted him the means to save Cardosia. The unreversed gift of her body in nurturing his child and delighting him in bed had lifted dark shadows he'd feared he'd live with for the rest of his life.

It was time to let go of the past. To embrace the challenges and rewards of the future.

On cue, his phone buzzed. He disentangled himself from his wife…his *wife*…chuckling when she protested in her sleep, and reached for it.

The message from Alessio removed all traces of amusement.

Rising, he fired back a response as he went into the bathroom. A quick shower later, he selected more formal attire than he'd worn in a while.

He was slipping on his favourite watch when he entered the bedroom.

'Why are you dressed? Are you leaving?' Her puzzled, sleep-roughened voice reached him from across the room.

He tensed, then forced calm into his body. Raising his head, he almost groaned at the sight of her. Tousled, sexy, a fertile goddess draped in tumbled white sheets that barely contained her beauty. The urge to tear his clothes off and slide beneath the covers with her was so strong, he had to mentally shake his head to regain his focus.

He was doing this for her.

For their child.

For Cardosia.

He couldn't lose sight of that. He'd tried to find a different solution, had fought the path he'd been urged to take for so long, but enough was enough. The critical mass had been reached. His uncle could no longer be allowed free rein.

'*Sì.* I have something to take care of.' He approached

the bed and leaned over, unable to help himself, to taste soft lips still swollen from his kisses. She blushed, still shy despite everything they'd done to each other in the last few days. Minutes later, he groaned and leaned his forehead against hers.

'I have to go, *dulce*. But you have two choices. I can send the chopper back to bring you home later or you can stay here. I'll be back tomorrow, maybe the day after.'

Her beautiful, astute eyes searched his. He knew she read in his eyes the resolution that pounded in his veins. After a handful of seconds, she nodded tentatively.

'I'll decide later. I have my laptop with me. I'll get some work done,' she replied.

Pride warred with this new extreme possessiveness he couldn't stem. He would be the last person to stand in the way of her work, but he didn't want her consumed with anything else but him. As irrational as that was.

'As long as you promise to take care of yourself?'

A slow smile spread across her face, the siren she was becoming rousing to render him even weaker. *'Sí, mi esposo,'* she responded with sultry seductiveness.

Dios mio. He shuddered to think how powerful she would be a year…ten years from now, when the shadows of desolation faded completely, and her confidence grew in spades.

Knowing he would be there to experience it set his veins alight. Just as her face, her body, her beautiful mind did.

With another, rougher groan, he tore himself away, stood looking down at her for an age before striding for the door. Teeth gritted, he grasped the handle, just as her voice reached him again.

'Seve?'

'*Sí*' He turned and froze.

She'd thrown off the sheet. One arm was flung above her head and her back arched ever so slightly, her blooming body on full seductive display. 'I'll miss you.'

'*Dulce cielo.*' As he pivoted and reversed direction, he knew he was going to be late.

Very late.

It was impossible to be this happy. Illogical, even. And yet here she was.

Delirious.

She'd taken her time to leave their bed after Seve's departure. She missed him even as he reluctantly dressed after ravishing her. Lingering in bed, breathing in his scent had made her heart swell even bigger. While she had reminders of him everywhere in the cabin, their bedroom was where she felt closest to him. So she'd stayed, lazily enjoying the breakfast tray delivered by the butler soon after Seve's chopper had taken off.

That was the other reason she'd stayed in bed. As she'd known he would, Seve had instructed the staff to descend on the cabin, his unapologetic protectiveness allowing no argument.

Well, she was just over eight months pregnant after all. So she'd gone from having just her husband for company to having a staff of six, including a doctor and two bodyguards, secreted in and around the cabin, keeping a discreet eye on her.

She sighed.

She wasn't really complaining. Seve was a busy man. A possessive one too, she was discovering. Why that sent a thrill through her, she wasn't going to question because she welcomed it. It fed a previously dried-up well where there should've been love and fulfilment but which instead was fractured with loneliness and desolation.

Which was why she was perfectly happy to dwell in her happy bubble all day and the next, taking a short walk to the wide, clear stream that ran a few hundred feet from the cabin. She even managed to ignore the guards who remained close but out of sight as she sat on a high rock next to the stream and raised her face to the warming sun.

Sadly, she couldn't outrun the chafing disquiet. And there by the stream, faint unease grew into a distinct pang.

She still hadn't told Seve she loved him. Because something was holding her back. Self-preservation because he hadn't expressed his own emotions?

Was she so shallow that she needed him to declare his feelings first?

The baby rolled as if mocking her. Genie smiled as she caressed her belly. 'The heart wants what it wants, doesn't it, darling?'

A firm kick. She laughed. Then slowly sobered.

What if Seve never said it? What if he was okay with the sex and the possessiveness and the whole Neanderthal hunter-gatherer moves but that was as far as it went? Would she be satisfied with that in the long term?

Her heart lurched.

No. She'd endured too much unhappiness to accept diluted devotion.

It was all or nothing. And if she had to fight for it…?

She pushed the thought away, rose and made her way

back to the cabin. Its solid ruggedness was reassuring, her fondness for the time she'd spent there blowing away the uncertainty as she stepped inside and followed the sounds and smells of cooking. Dinner was an hour away but her walk had made her peckish.

Conversation stopped when she walked into the kitchen.

The guard and butler from the estate, who'd made an appearance with the rest of the staff, murmured greetings. But she knew something else was going on, couldn't miss the excitement in the air.

'What's going on?'

Both men appeared hesitant. But Sofia, elbow-deep in flour, looked up, her eyes shining. 'It's the *señor*. He's making the announcement. Finally.'

Finally.

One simple word. And yet it sent icy cold shivers racing over her body.

'Wh-what do you mean?'

The housekeeper, clueless to the speaking glances being cast her way by the men in the room, continued, 'It's on all the TV, *señora*. Do you want to see?' She nodded to the tablet set on the kitchen island, but the butler stepped forward.

'Or perhaps I can get you something to eat, *señora*?' he said.

Her appetite gone, Genie shook her head. 'No, I want to see.'

Her shaky voice gave her away. Sofia's excitement dropped, her eyes widening as she finally read the room. Before she could speak, Genie snatched up the tablet.

Her first thought was that it was a good thing she

could speak Cardosian. The second was that it wouldn't have mattered at all because the press conference was large enough to convey the importance of the event. Not to mention the helpful subtitles running along the bottom of the screen that screamed *Breaking News!* with a countdown clock promising said news in less than three minutes.

The venue was the Cardosian Parliament Building.

And there was Seve Valente, her husband, his features stamped with fierce intent as Alfredo Santiago wrapped up his heralding speech.

Rousing words flew from the older man's lips.

'Self-made billionaire… Beloved by his people… A selfless Cardosian with his people's interests at heart who returned home to devote himself to his country. A newly minted husband with a child on the way. Everything Lorenzo Valente was not and would never be!'

The rush of blood in her ears almost drowned out Santiago's voice. But the subtitles kept coming. Wave after wave of dread inundated Genie. She vaguely registered concerned voices and firm hands taking hold of her, hustling her out of the kitchen and into the living room. But she still didn't let go of the tablet. Or take her gaze off Seve.

Behind him were some of the men who'd attended her wedding. Men she recollected had been part of his uncle's administration. And to the side, looking almost cynically amused but for his equally calculating expression, was Alessio Montaldi.

Her gaze returned to Seve, her heart hammering harder as she refocused on his face, his words. As he announced that, following his uncle's resignation, he was standing for president.

To his credit—or by design—he didn't viciously malign his uncle. Hell, he barely mentioned him at all. And perhaps she would've forgiven him, had the lingering niggle not finally revealed itself as the betrayal she'd subconsciously feared as Seve stared into the camera and delivered his speech.

'Cardosia deserves a different vision. A better vision. The road ahead is tough and will require difficult choices, hard work and sacrifice. I'm not a stranger to any of those things.' He stared into the middle distance for a moment, shadows crossing his face before he refocused. 'Challenges will arise and seek to derail us. I've had a few of my own recently. But we will meet those challenges and turn them into advantage.' The crowd roared until he raised an imperious hand. 'You will be pleased to know I've already started the groundwork…'

The rush in her ears grew louder.

The groundwork…

Her algorithm? Their marriage? *Their baby?*

As the vice around her heart tightened, Genie registered that she wasn't even upset that Seve had procured the algorithm as a stepping stone to gain political power. She knew first-hand that her algorithm would do good.

But he'd deliberately kept her in the dark about his end goal—usurping power from his uncle. Using her as part of his plan to take his ultimate revenge. While she'd been gleefully basking in happy ever afters and love and family, he'd been scheming on how to turn the accidental pregnancy of his one-night stand into political gain.

Everything had been one giant ploy orchestrated by Seve to get her onside.

Her vision went ashen.

Sofia made a distressed sound and pressed a glass of water into her shaky hand. When she pushed it away, shaking her head, dizziness washed over her.

Then a wave of darkness swept it all away.

CHAPTER ELEVEN

'THIS WASN'T WHAT we agreed.'

Seve had said that a few times and was well aware he was repeating himself. Could he blame the euphoric catharsis of finally confronting his uncle and driving the old man out of his life as an excuse for being swept into a hasty decision? One he'd made without consulting the most important person in his life?

'We needed to seize the momentum. Strike while the iron was hot.'

Alessio quirked an eyebrow at Alfredo Santiago from across the room. 'Any more idioms up your sleeve you wish to toss in, old man?'

Seve glared at his friend, then transferred his gaze to the minister who'd orchestrated the press conference without Seve's approval.

'That wasn't how I planned on doing things, Santiago.'

Santiago managed to look contrite for a moment. But he perked up a moment later. *'Sí, el presidente.'*

'Don't call me that.'

Santiago snorted, contrition replaced by ebullience. 'Did you not hear them out there? They're ecstatic. The polls are on fire for you and the stock markets are already trending upwards. This is the best news our country has had in decades. Why aren't you celebrating?'

One word came to mind.

Genie.

He'd gone about this all wrong. While others were to blame for jumping the gun a little, he'd taken the familiar route of playing his cards close to his chest when the very person who was responsible for him finally taking the right action was kept in the dark.

This life he was leading wasn't about him any more. He'd known that in the weeks he'd spent on tenterhooks waiting for Genie to accept his proposal. In the visceral soul-connection he'd felt with her since he brought her to Cardosia.

I should've told her many more things. Like I love her.

Something shook to vicious life in him.

There it was. The final puzzle piece he'd been looking for since he could remember. The one thing that made utter and complete sense. The one thing his billions couldn't buy.

He strode from his desk to wide windows in the minister's office. Behind him puzzled silence reigned.

They didn't know. They probably never would if they weren't as lucky as him.

But had he gambled with that luck with his actions? A strain of terror so debilitating gripped him he had trouble digging for his phone.

'*Señor?*'

'It's time to leave, gentlemen,' Alessio said. 'The circus is over for now. Give the man some space.'

'But—'

'I must insist,' Alessio intoned, his tone coated in titanium.

This was why he was his friend. Why Seve had trusted no one but him with the final investigation into his uncle, ensuring Lorenzo didn't get away with any more atrocities. Alessio Montaldi was a man of many dark and dubious talents.

'You want me to stay?' Alessio asked once the room had cleared.

Seve sensed his friend's restlessness. Hell, he was surprised the Sicilian had returned considering the situation *he* had brewing back in Europe.

'No. I'll handle it from here, *gracias*,' he said, despite the dreadful weight in his stomach that said he'd screwed up. Big time.

He'd emancipated himself from the dark shadows of the past. Finally.

'We may bear the same surname, but I will never call you family. You're out of my life for good.'

Lorenzo had had the audacity to looked shocked at Seve's parting words. But in putting his past ghosts to rest, had he thrown his future into jeopardy?

Alessio clasped him on the shoulder. *'Buena fortuna*, friend. You know where to find me if you need me.'

He nodded but barely heard his friend leave. His heart was stuttering in his chest as he listened to the phone ring and ring and *ring*.

The past twenty-four hours had been beyond hectic, but he'd received reports that Genie was fine. She'd chosen to stay at the cabin instead of returning to the estate.

So why wasn't she answering?

He redialled his security, every bone in his body locking when that phone too rang endlessly. About to give up, he exhaled in relief when it was answered.

Then he was grateful for the glass wall's support as

the strength leached from his body. 'Repeat that,' he snapped, one hand braced against the window.

'I'm sorry, *señor*. But your wife fell unconscious. The doctor is with her. We're about to board the helicopter—'

'What happened?' he shouted, terror eating him alive. The urgent voices in the background made his fingers tighten on the phone and his stomach churn.

'She was watching your press conference, *señor*. And she got a little distressed.'

Horror dredged harder through him. 'Is she…is she okay?'

Genie was strong. Wilful. Highly intelligent. And utterly beautiful. But so far she'd fainted at one other key moment. When she'd discovered she was pregnant with his child. How utterly idiotic of him to believe he could make such life-changing decisions without considering how it would affect the most important person in his life.

'*Señor?*'

He powered through the soul-shrivelling self-recrimination to focus on the voice seeking his attention. The doctor. 'What's wrong with her?'

'I don't know for sure yet, sir. Her vitals are a little erratic so I think it's best she's taken to the hospital.'

'Where are you taking her?'

'The private facility where the birth was to take place is best.'

'*Dios mio.* The baby…'

His recklessness might have put not just his wife but his child in danger.

For eight incredible days, he'd had everything he wanted. Had he thrown it away with his recklessness?

No. Not while he had breath in his body.

'I'll meet you there.'

He hung up and sprinted for the door, startling the small crowd gathered outside.

'Get the hell out of my way,' he snarled when one brave soul attempted to approach.

But even as he staggered out of the building and attempted not to bellow his agony, he knew the totality of the anger and guilt he felt was directed at himself. Just as he knew should anything happen to his wife, he would never be the same.

The swim up to consciousness was long and terribly unpleasant.

Genie knew something awaited her. Something that would set her back months, *years*, throw her back to the place she feared and detested most.

Loneliness. Desolation. Despair.

And this time, it would be a million times worse. Because now she knew the difference between pure love and parental indifference and selfishness. She'd scaled the ultimate high. Now she was heading for the darkest low.

The machines continued to beep, diligently dragging her from the shadows, beep by beep into the light of false hope.

'Turn it off,' she mumbled, as if by the sheer act of speaking the words, she'd get her wish and return to sweet oblivion.

But when had any wish of hers been truly granted? She'd believed in a false fairy tale with nothing but disappointment on the last page.

A sob caught in her throat. A rough sound echoed in the room.

It took several moments to realise the other noise didn't come from her.

Seve?

No. He was busy turning *his* dream into reality. He'd plotted his fairy tale with no mistakes or flaws. Unlike her.

'*Dios mio, mi amor.* Don't cry.' The far too familiar voice, deep and low, last heard whispering incredibly sensual words in her ear as he made her soar with bliss.

Blissed out and ignorant.

'Don't tell me what to do,' she mumbled around a constricted throat. 'You should leave. I don't want you here.'

Another sound, much like jagged anguish, echoed again. 'Open your eyes, Genie.'

The punch of steely authority almost made her chuckle. Which was the height of absurdity. Maybe they'd given her meds that were making her delirious.

Would they though, considering she was…?

Her baby!

Her hand launched off the bed, another sob crowding her throat when she touched the hard, full swell of her belly, more tears, this time of relief, pouring from beneath her eyelids.

'The baby is fine, *pequeña.* Healthy and doing well. But please. Open your eyes. Let me see that you're okay.' One warm hand gripped the hand not on her belly.

She snatched it away. 'I'm not okay. But that's none of your business. Not any more. Go away.'

More sounds that were a weird mix of aggravation and misery drifted low over her ravaged senses.

Seve was there, yes, but perhaps the sounds were from Lita?

The old woman must be distressed by the possibility of her great-grandchild in distress. Genie wanted to open her eyes and reassure her but she was terrified because Seve was here, too. Even now, through the beeping and desolation and utter hopelessness, her awareness of him was insane.

She wasn't ready to face what the rest of her life looked like. Not yet. Maybe her instincts had been safeguarding her from this by keeping her unconscious. Because the sharpness of the agony was unbearable.

So she turned her head away.

The baby was fine. Somehow, she believed Seve when he said *that*.

Everything else, she would deal with…later.

'What do you mean there's nothing wrong with her? My wife is in a hospital bed. She won't talk or eat more than a few bites of food!'

Seve was aware his attitude was terrifying the staff. Prowling up and down the halls of the private hospital sent people scurrying for cover.

He didn't care.

All he cared about was Genie. Who'd been hospitalised for a week and had barely spoken a word to him. Or Lita. Or her doctors.

When she'd finally opened her eyes, the sheer misery and desolation in the blue depths had taken him out at the knees. Hell, he'd half wished she'd remained sleeping because he never wanted to see that expression again. Especially knowing he was the cause of it.

But any attempt to talk to her had been met with

silence and apathy. It was the apathy that was driving him insane. The woman he knew fought tooth and nail for the smallest cause.

That he was responsible for her dejection terrified him more than he was willing to admit.

It didn't help that Lita, keeping vigil outside Genie's room, glared at him with unabashed recrimination every chance she got.

'We were a little worried about her blood pressure but that's stabilised in the last few days,' the doctor said.

'So what's wrong with my wife now? Why can't I take her home?' he pressed, that ever-growing stone of terror in his gut crushing the life out of him.

The short, bespectacled doctor squirmed for a minute before sighing. 'We've already discussed this with Mrs Valente. She's aware she can leave but she…indicated that she would rather remain here.'

A lesser man would've reeled from the shock. Seve clenched his gut and called on every ounce of self-control, past, present, and future, to keep him from crumbling.

'If there's nothing else, *señor*?'

The moment he dismissed him, the doctor scurried away, leaving Seve staring at the swinging door to the private waiting room.

He faintly registered that the hand he was dragging through his hair was shaking. Hell, his whole body was shaking.

Genie would rather remain within the soulless grey walls of a hospital than return home?

Grey walls…like her tech dungeon? Had he ruined things so spectacularly that his wife preferred the desolation of her past life?

Before unwanted answers could eviscerate him, he was striding down the hall.

He'd just reached her room when his hand was snagged in a firm hold. He glanced down at his grandmother, impatience rifling through him.

'Lita, I need—'

'I know what you need,' she said in a firm, urgent voice. 'And *I* need you to understand that the only way forward is to truly open your heart. Show her who you truly are. I want to go home, *mijo*, and I'd really like to take my family with me.'

Seve nodded, the rock in his throat preventing him from speaking.

Resolution pounding through his blood, he opened the door to Genie's room.

She'd showered recently. Her drying hair was brushed and hung around her shoulders, and she was propped up by several pillows. The scent of her shampoo hit him and he curled his fingers against the desperate urge to stride over to the bed, scoop her up in his arms and bury his face in her throat until the world stopped its insane spinning.

Instead, he stood there, enduring her dismissive silence, until, perhaps sensing his intent, she angled her head towards him.

'Seve.'

His name on her lips punched him hard in the gut. 'Yes. You want me to go away. But I'm not leaving. Not today, not ever.'

She stiffened and cast him a look filled with misery and a fraction of the fire she usually showed. But it was fire, nonetheless. And it gave him much-needed impetus.

'I screwed up. Big time. I know. But, *mi amor*—'

'I'm not your *amor*. If you care even a little bit about me, you'll stop calling me that.'

'You are so I won't.'

She inhaled, shakily at first, then she rallied, her fingers linking under her extended belly. Like the exquisite goddess she was, her chin tilted upward, her eyes glancing over him before she looked at a point over his shoulder. 'I'm not going to debate that with you. It's not worth my time.'

He sighed. Ventured closer. 'Why haven't you touched your laptop?' he asked, nudging a chin at the neglected gadget on her bedside table.

She cast an uninterested glance at her favourite device and shrugged despondently. 'Nothing on there that can't wait.'

'Wait for what exactly? For me to do as you wish and leave? Because, in case you didn't hear me, I'm not going.'

'Then what do you want?'

'For you to come home. With me. With Lita.'

Her chin wobbled for a handful of seconds before she controlled it. 'I don't have a home, not any more. I probably never did.'

'You did. You do. Always.'

Another wave of pain, then she shook her head. 'Don't you have a *presidency* to step into?'

The word was a curse that flayed his skin. Deservedly. Teeth gritted, he replied, 'No, I don't.'

Surprise slid through the despair. 'What do you mean? I saw you and your people on TV making an announcement. Proudly citing your *groundwork* and how you turned your recent challenges into advantages.

Tell me you didn't mean me. That you didn't mean our baby?' she shot at him, daring him to refute it.

Shame gripped him, the ground beneath his feet shifting dangerously. 'I did,' he confessed gruffly.

Her pale face whitened and he cursed himself to hell. 'Genie—'

'No. No more. I can't...' Her voice wobbled but she rallied. 'It may not have been part of your plan, but you used me...us...as a tool to battle your uncle, didn't you?'

His jaw clenched. 'Not as a tool. As an armour. My armour. Because that's what you've been for me.'

She laughed and his insides ripped to shreds at the bitterness he heard. 'That's great for you, I guess. But using me as your armour left *me* vulnerable. Do you know how it feels to know you didn't want me or a child but used us anyway because you saw us as an *opportunity*?'

He rushed forward, then stopped at the foot of her bed. It wouldn't do to rush this, as much as he wanted to. He needed to explain himself. 'That's not true. I've wanted you from the moment I saw you.'

Her lips turned down. 'Well, I'm glad it all worked out for you, Seve...' She paused, a wave of pain washing over her face before she shook her head.

He braced his hands on the footboard. 'Just before our wedding I got wind that my uncle was striking a half-a-trillion-dollar deal to sell off every single diamond mine in Cardosia to a foreign government. If it had gone through, the country would've been begging for scraps from other nations for the next five generations. I couldn't let that happen.' He paused, took a breath. 'I couldn't let what he did to me go unanswered either. I needed to confront him. On all fronts.'

A sliver of softness washed over her face, but she still shook her head. 'I get that. But I had to find out via the news. And what Santiago said, about you becoming a family man giving you the advantage... It all sounded so calculating.'

'It was mistimed, misguided and not at all what I intended when I left you that morning, *pequeña*.'

'But you happen to have the very tools you need,' she replied, scathing condemnation in her voice. 'How very convenient.'

'If you're talking about the presidency, Santiago is about to announce that it was all a misunderstanding. I've told him to withdraw my name with immediate effect.'

Shock widened her eyes. 'You have?'

'I told you. All this snowballed out of control before I could stop it.'

'So you don't want to be president?'

Unable to resist, he crept closer and perched on the edge of her bed.

This close, her scent washed over him, renewing him as surely as food and water. 'I never wanted the position. And especially not if it drove you away. You're the most important thing in my life, Genie. You and our baby. And don't forget, I have an insanely successful venture capitalist empire to run. I know you feel I've betrayed and used you and our baby, but I meant what I said. You empowered me to do what I should've done two decades ago. To stand up to my uncle, and not let his brutality shadow my life. I love my country but, before I brought you here, I only helped it from afar because the memories were too harrowing for me. You deserved better than a man stuck in the past, residing in bitterness, licking his wounds. I wanted to give that to you.'

'You didn't have to fight him alone.'

'It's a flaw I will work on, but I'm used to doing things on my own. Genie, you conquered your demons long ago. I was ashamed I'd let mine get the better of me for so long. I wanted to make myself whole. For you.'

Her nostrils quivered but again she shook her head, terrifying him even more. 'Don't you see? You were always whole to me. Our scars remind us of what we've been through. How far we've come. They're what make you the man I…'

His heart lurched when she stopped. 'The man you what, Genie?'

'It doesn't matter. Not any more.'

His fists bunched but he forced himself to relax them. 'Please, my love. Forgive me. I'm so used to doing things on my own. I've been so busy fighting to make things right in Cardosia that I didn't stop to consider what this would do to you. To us. But what you've shown me these past few months… I never want to jeopardise that.' He sucked in a deep breath and reached out to cup her delicate jaw. 'I love you.'

A shudder ran through her, and she visibly shook as she inhaled. 'You do?'

'*Dulce cielo, si*. With everything inside me. I worship the ground you walk on, *mi amor*. That incredible brain of yours. This insane body nurturing our child. You're everything to me.'

'Oh, Seve. I thought… I thought…'

'I know what you thought. I swear I will never betray or mislead you.'

Wide beautiful eyes stared up at him. 'I was crushed,

Seve. After everything we've been through, I felt like an afterthought. I never want to feel like that again.'

He swallowed as he leaned forward and brushed her lips with his. 'I'm sorry. Forgive me.'

Her hands rose to grip his wrists and she nodded. 'Yes.'

Joy tore through him. But as he went to kiss her again, she placed a finger on his lips. 'I think this is where you ask me why I was so crushed.'

He frowned. 'What?'

She rolled her eyes. 'I love you too, Seve. Only love can make things hurt this deeply. I've been in love with you for weeks. Months. I've been dying to tell you, but I think I needed to hear how you felt first, just in case—'

'*Te quiero mucho. Siempre.* You never need to wonder again.'

A long, moan-filled kiss later, he pulled back. 'Have mercy and tell me I can take you home now? Before Lita sends in the army?'

Her smile sucked the air from his lungs. Dear God, she was so beautiful.

And mine.

'Yes,' she said simply.

Rising, he plucked the phone and called his driver. Then he whirled around as Genie made a choking sound. She was standing next to the bed, clutching her belly.

'Oh…oh, my God! I think Lita's going to have to wait a little longer.'

His lungs emptied as a new burst of terror exploded in his chest. Tossing the phone aside, he gripped her arms. 'Why? Tell me what's happening, Genie,' he rasped, his voice breaking with the fear pulsing through him

Her eyes filled with trepidation…and wonder. Then, miraculously, another smile that set his world to rights. 'Seve…the baby… I think it's coming.'

He shook his head fiercely, as if the act could reverse her words. 'But…it can't. You have two more weeks…'

'I don't think our baby wants to wait that long.'

'Dios mio,' he muttered, then bellowed for the doctor.

A long time later, he would wonder how he'd managed to keep breathing. To keep reasoning. To keep from losing his mind when every cell in his body was either frozen in shock or marvelling at the strength his wife possessed.

Because watching Genie bring their daughter into the world floored him and changed him on a fundamental level he never wanted to reverse.

Seve knew he held on because her eyes were no longer shuttered. They blazed with love and determination and power.

For him.

For their baby the moment she was placed in her arms.

He was a risk-taker who'd come within a whisker of losing the most important thing in his life.

'What are you thinking?' Her voice was a little hoarse from her labour but all the more breathtaking for it.

He looked up from the sheer wonder of his beautiful daughter, Angelina Valente, into the equally captivating face of his wife. The woman who owned his very existence. 'Promise me you'll never let me screw this up? If

I come within a whisker of making you or our children unhappy, you make my life hell until I fix it. Promise.'

Tears filled her eyes and spilled over but the smile that bloomed on her face made his heart swell so big he was terrified it would burst. 'I promise,' she whispered, then held out her arms.

He walked into them willingly, placed their baby back in her arms before enfolding them close.

'*Dios mio*, I love you. Both of you. So much.'

'*Yo también, mi corazón,*' she whispered. Then she raised her face to his. 'Now kiss me, my darling husband. Then take us home.'

* * * * *

Did Pregnant and Stolen by the Tycoon
leave you craving more?
Then make sure to check out these other
irresistible stories by Maya Blake!

Bound by Her Rival's Baby
A Vow to Claim His Hidden Son
Their Desert Night of Scandal
His Pregnant Desert Queen
The Greek's Forgotten Marriage

Available now!

#4153 THE MAID'S PREGNANCY BOMBSHELL
Cinderella Sisters for Billionaires
by Lynne Graham
Shy hotel maid Alana is so desperate to clear a family debt that when she discovers Greek tycoon Ares urgently needs a wife, she blurts out a scandalous suggestion: *she'll* become his convenient bride. But as chemistry blazes between them, she has an announcement that will inconveniently disrupt his well-ordered world... She's having his baby!

#4154 A BILLION-DOLLAR HEIR FOR CHRISTMAS
by Caitlin Crews
When Tiago Villela discovers Lillie Merton is expecting, a wedding is nonnegotiable. To protect the Villela billions, his child must be legitimate. But his plan for a purely pragmatic arrangement is soon threatened by a dangerously insatiable desire...

#4155 A CHRISTMAS CONSEQUENCE FOR THE GREEK
Heirs to a Greek Empire
by Lucy King
Booking billionaire Zander's birthday is a triumph for caterer Mia. And the hottest thing on the menu? A scorching one-night stand! But a month later, he can't be reached. Mia finally ambushes him at work to reveal she's pregnant! He insists she move in with him, but this Christmas she wants all or nothing!

#4156 MISTAKEN AS HIS ROYAL BRIDE
Princess Brides for Royal Brothers
by Abby Green
Maddi hadn't fully considered the implications of posing as her secret half sister. *Or* that King Aristedes would demand she continue the pretense as his intended bride. Immersing herself in the royal life she was denied growing up is as compelling as it is daunting. But so is the thrill of Aristedes's smoldering gaze...

#4157 VIRGIN'S STOLEN NIGHTS WITH THE BOSS
Heirs to the Romero Empire
by Carol Marinelli

Polo player Elias rarely spares a glance for his staff, until he meets stable hand and former heiress Carmen. And their attraction is irresistible! Elias knows he'll give the innocent all the pleasure she could want, but that's it. Unless their passion can unlock a connection much harder to walk away from...

#4158 CROWNED FOR THE KING'S SECRET
Behind the Palace Doors...
by Kali Anthony

One year ago, her spine-tingling night with exiled king Sandro left Victoria pregnant and alone. Lied to by the palace, she believed he wanted nothing to do with them. So Sandro turning up on her doorstep—ready to claim her, his heir and his kingdom—is astounding!

#4159 HIS INNOCENT UNWRAPPED IN ICELAND
by Jackie Ashenden

Orion North wants Isla's company...and her! So when the opportunity to claim both at the convenient altar arises, he takes it. But with tragedy in his past, even their passion may not be enough to melt the ice encasing his heart...

#4160 THE CONVENIENT COSENTINO WIFE
by Jane Porter

Clare Redmond retreated from the world, pregnant and grieving her fiancé's death, never expecting to see his ice-cold brother, Rocco, again. She's stunned when the man who always avoided her storms back into her life, demanding they wed to give her son the life a Cosentino deserves!

YOU CAN FIND MORE INFORMATION ON UPCOMING HARLEQUIN TITLES, FREE EXCERPTS AND MORE AT HARLEQUIN.COM.

HPCNMRB1023

Get 3 FREE REWARDS!

We'll send you 2 FREE Books plus a FREE Mystery Gift.

FREE Value Over $20

Both the **Harlequin® Desire** and **Harlequin Presents®** series feature compelling novels filled with passion, sensuality and intriguing scandals.

YES! Please send me 2 FREE novels from the Harlequin Desire or Harlequin Presents series and my FREE gift (gift is worth about $10 retail). After receiving them, if I don't wish to receive any more books, I can return the shipping statement marked "cancel." If I don't cancel, I will receive 6 brand-new Harlequin Presents Larger-Print books every month and be billed just $6.30 each in the U.S. or $6.49 each in Canada, a savings of at least 10% off the cover price, or 3 Harlequin Desire books (2-in-1 story editions) every month and be billed just $7.83 each in the U.S. or $8.43 each in Canada, a savings of at least 12% off the cover price. It's quite a bargain! Shipping and handling is just 50¢ per book in the U.S. and $1.25 per book in Canada.* I understand that accepting the 2 free books and gift places me under no obligation to buy anything. I can always return a shipment and cancel at any time by calling the number below. The free books and gift are mine to keep no matter what I decide.

Choose one: ☐ **Harlequin Desire**
(225/326 BPA GRNA)

☐ **Harlequin Presents Larger-Print**
(176/376 BPA GRNA)

☐ **Or Try Both!**
(225/326 & 176/376 BPA GRQP)

Name (please print)

Address   Apt. #

City   State/Province   Zip/Postal Code

Email: Please check this box ☐ if you would like to receive newsletters and promotional emails from Harlequin Enterprises ULC and its affiliates. You can unsubscribe anytime.

Mail to the **Harlequin Reader Service:**
IN U.S.A.: P.O. Box 1341, Buffalo, NY 14240-8531
IN CANADA: P.O. Box 603, Fort Erie, Ontario L2A 5X3

Want to try 2 free books from another series! Call 1-800-873-8635 or visit www.ReaderService.com.

HDHP23